D1135186

The Baron and the Stolen Legacy

THE BARON
and
THE STOLEN LEGACY

BY

John Creasey

AS

Anthony Morton

CHARLES SCRIBNER'S SONS

c 1962

New York

89B4390

CONTENTS

I

TRUE VALUE

THE girl approached Mannering, obviously young, eager and happy, and she made all the assistants in the shop turn to look at her—even Josh Larraby, the manager. The shop itself, Quinns, was nearly four hundred years old, and Mannering dealt mostly in antiques and *objets d'art*, old paintings and jewellery. True, modern jewellery sometimes came his way but it did not greatly interest him, whereas everything old or ancient attracted and sometimes fascinated him.

It was impossible to think of this girl against a background of age. She belonged to today, with her short and narrow skirt and nicely rounded legs, the jumper pulled on as if carelessly over brown hair that was a little untidy, and a bosom with more promise than maturity. The shop was always kept in a subdued light, with clear brightness only at certain points to aid prospective customers to make up their minds, and the girl seemed to bring the sunlight with her. Outside, in Hart Row, Mayfair, the sun was shining with all the deceptive brilliance of an English spring.

Tom Wainwright walked behind the girl, hurrying, as if finding it difficult to keep pace. She kept her eyes on Mannering, obviously realising who he was, as obviously liking what she saw.

She stopped. "Are you Mr. John Mannering?"

"Yes," answered Mannering. "And you're Rebecca Blest."

"Yes, I am." She took his hand, and hers was slim, cool and firm; his engulfed it. As soon as she let his go, she slid the strap of a bag off her shoulder; her eyes seemed to dance with delight. "I've got them here. I thought it

7

would be safer to carry them casually than to look as if I had a fortune with me."

"Very wise, too," approved Mannering, mildly. He glanced over her head. "All right, Tom. Come in, Miss Blest." He stood aside for her to enter his small office, the shelves crowded with leather-bound reference books and catalogues, a Queen Anne bow fronted desk at one side, with William and Mary slung chairs in front of it. In one corner, concealed by the bookshelves, was the entrance to the strong rooms, and although Rebecca Blest almost certainly did not realise it, in those strong rooms were jewels and other valuables worth nearly a million pounds. "Sit down," invited Mannering, and moved a chair a few inches.

The girl held the large black plastic bag in both hands, rather like an offering, until he had rounded the desk to his own chair. Then, her eyes brimming over with high spirits and excitement, she placed it in front of him; only then did she sit down.

"There!" she said, as if a tremendous task had been accomplished. "Mr. Mannering—" she broke off.

"Yes?"

"The man I telephoned at Sotheby's said that I couldn't find a better valuer than you for these."

"That was nice of him, but you shouldn't take even Sotheby's compliments for granted," Mannering said drily. "Have you any idea what they're worth?"

She didn't answer, but seemed to catch her breath.

"None at all?" encouraged Mannering.

She said: "I just daren't guess. I daren't. When I heard about the legacy, I mean the inheritance, I just— well, it was like winning a sweepstake prize. At least I suppose that's what it feels like, I've never had any luck, but—well, I just daren't guess." She bit her lips. "My father says—"

She broke off.

"Yes?"

"It's ridiculous, but he says twenty or thirty thousand

pounds. It can't be so much." Now she was speaking very hurriedly, and was breathless. "He would have come with me this afternoon if he'd been well enough, but the doctor advised him not to get up for a few more days. He had a mild coronary." Anxiety showed through her expression momentarily. "Thank God he won't have to worry about working any more." She paused again, and then burst out: "Please look at them, and put me out of my misery."

"Is there a key?"

"It's not locked," Rebecca Blest said.

Mannering chuckled, and she also laughed, but on a rather high-pitched note. Mannering decided not to keep her on tenterhooks any longer.

He knew only that she had telephoned him this morning about the jewels, with a story of an unexpected inheritance. He had checked the story and had it confirmed. She lived in a Notting Hill flatlet with her father; they made just enough money to live comfortably. Apparently three deaths in the family over a period of two years had made Samuel Blest the sole legatee of a distant relative's estate. The estate included a house in Barnes, in poor condition, and let on lease; the furniture wasn't anything to write home about, according to his informant. But the jewellery, handed down from generation to generation, should be worth a fortune.

Mannering opened the black bag. Inside were the oddments one would expect to find in a young woman's handbag, as well as a brown paper parcel, too large for the inner section. He smothered a grin as he took this out, but he had often found a fortune in precious stones wrapped up in a rag and a few bits of cotton wool, so this didn't surprise him. He placed the parcel carefully in front of him. It was fairly well-packed, and soft to the touch—it was in fact cotton wool. Someone had advised the girl well on packing, or else the inheritance had always been kept like this. Old men with a fortune in jewels tucked away often treated them as if they were junk.

Mannering began to unpick the knot, and the girl burst out:

"Oh, *cut* it!"

Mannering opened a pen-knife, and did what he was told, then began to put the smaller packets on the desk in front of him. Each piece of jewellery was wrapped in cotton wool, and the wool had a grubby look, as if it had been handled time and time again. There were seventeen small packs in all, seventeen pieces—necklaces, clips, ear-rings, and such-like, no doubt; all the variety one would expect. Mildly intrigued by the girl's anxiety, and not even vaguely suspicious that all was not what it seemed, he unwrapped the largest of the packets. He could feel the hardness of the settings through the cotton wool as he unfolded it, and glimpsed the gold two or three times before he realised the truth.

This was not old gold which had been worked by crafts-men centuries ago; this piece was set in the modern method, with a perfunctory if crafty imitation of the old. He looked down, putting it to one side; it was a bracelet, and there seemed little doubt that the girl believed the stones in it to be diamonds.

They were paste, not even of the quality which would deceive the expert for a while.

"Well?" Rebecca Blest exclaimed.

Mannering said: "Give me a few minutes, Miss Blest," and unwrapped another packet, this time a necklace; then two brooches, and a tiny packet which contained four rings. Here were imitation diamonds, imitation rubies, sapphires, emeralds, and here were cultured pearls. The collection on his desk grew quickly, each piece resting on its own bed of grubby cotton wool, and the girl began to shift in her chair, she was so anxious for his pronounce-ment.

He did not at all relish what he had to do; it was like taking sweets from a child. Yet he had no choice. Now and again he had glanced at her, and he wondered whether she already had some inkling of what he was going to tell her; certainly something of her excitement had faded, but that could be because she was impatient. He pushed his chair back a few inches, rested his hands on the desk, and studied her. Yes, she was beginning to feel uneasy. Her lips were no longer parted in eagerness, but tightly set. Her eyes had lost some of their bright blue brilliance, and she was clasping her hands in her lap.

"Rebecca," he said, very quietly, "these aren't what you thought they were."

She didn't say a word.

"I hate to tell you," Mannering went on, "but you have to know sooner or later. These are paste gems, and the settings are of modern make. They're not worth much, I'm afraid."

She moistened her lips. Her eyes seemed to grow very large and round, then she closed them and screwed them up as if to fight back tears. Mannering saw the tautness of her fingers, where they were interlocked.

"I'm really sorry," Mannering said. "Of course, they're worth a bit." He was the incurable romantic, as the portrait on the wall above his head showed; in it, he was dressed as a Cavalier, with all the furbelows of the time. His wife had painted that, to catch the spirit of the man: the good-looks, the hazel brown eyes, the clear-cut features—the man sitting at the desk seemed rather like a reincarnation of the one in the portrait. He made a quick estimate of the value of the costume jewellery, which on the right woman would look very well. If he averaged it at twenty pounds a piece, it would be generous; three hundred and forty pounds or so. "In fact I could buy it from you at five hundred pounds."

She opened her eyes, but did not speak; it was as if the shock of disappointment had made her dumb.

"Or perhaps you want to keep it, for sentimental reasons," he said. "I shall quite understand—"

"*Sent*iment!" she cried. "Sentiment!" She pushed her chair back and stood up, as if she needed some kind of release from tension and could not sit still any longer.

"No, we're not interested in sentimental value. My father *hates* the family."

She broke off, but it was obviously no moment for Mannering to speak, and he watched as she stared at a small gilded cross, brought to him by a cleric from Italy, then at the spines of the books, then up at his portrait; she stared at that for a moment, but it did not hold her interest. She had her arms rigid by her sides now, her hands clenched.

". . . Oh, what's the use of getting worked up?" she said at last, and momentarily closed her eyes again. "Did you say five hundred pounds?"

"Yes."

"Couldn't you—couldn't you make it more?"

"I'm afraid not," Mannering said, and wondered if there was any special reason for her wanting another hundred or two. "When I've had a closer look at it I might find one or two of the pieces better than I think they are."

She said: "Yes, I suppose so. I suppose I could—I could take them to someone else."

He smiled. "By all means." He hoped that she wouldn't, being quite sure that she would get no more than half his offer, and having a feeling that if she discovered that he had acted on an impulse of romantic generosity, she would become suddenly, perhaps, haughtily, proud. "I'm really sorry, Miss Blest, but—"

She stared up at the portrait again.

"I can't understand it," she said. "I just can't understand it. It's almost as if he had stretched out from the grave to hurt my father."

Mannering murmured: "Who did?" and wondered how much truth there was in the story of the three deaths which had led her father to the inheritance. It seemed certain that she believed it. There was someone in the family whom she had good reason to dislike, and the whole story might well be worth the hearing. His thoughts began to wander. Had the previous owner had these replicas of real gems made, and sold the genuine ones? Had owner 1, 2 or 3 carried out the switch? Had any of the other inheritors, in their lifetime, discovered the switch from real to false?

Had the switch been done recently?

These and a lot of other questions chased one another through his mind as Mannering watched the girl. As far as he could judge, the false gems had been in those settings for some years, for nothing suggested brand new work and each piece needed cleaning. At the simplest, this was a matter for the insurance company, but insurance liability was in turn a matter for experts and not for him; he wished only that he could help this girl.

She was staring at him intently.

"My Uncle Rett did."

"Your Uncle Rett."

"The uncle who died—" she broke off, and turned away again. "Oh, it's such a long story, and it's hopelessly involved. My father's brother-in-law, Rett Larker, inherited the jewels and everything else, and he left everything to my father. If Uncle Rett had wanted to hurt, he couldn't have chosen a better way." The girl had a scared look, now. "I don't know how this will affect my father," she confided, and approached the desk with one hand outstretched as if in appeal. "I think the shock might harm him. He—he's been so ill."

Now both her hands were stretched out to Mannering. There was no doubt of the intensity of her pleading. He could go up to seven hundred; it had been a good year, and the loss could be absorbed—but only a fool would consider it.

"Need you tell him?" she demanded. "Can you give me a letter, or a valuation, or even something which says you have to take some time to get an accurate valuation? Something I can show my father and make him think it's all right, that it's only a matter of time."

"But would that help?" asked Mannering.

"Yes, of course it would," Rebecca Blest declared. "It—

it would let him down much more lightly. I could—I could tell him the truth gradually, and he needn't know the whole truth until he's much stronger. Will you help me?"

It would have taken a much harder-hearted man to tell her no. And because he wanted to know if she went to someone else, Mannering sent his most agile assistant after her.

2

PAIN DEFERRED . . .

REBECCA BLEST turned out of Hart Row into Bond Street, Mayfair, only vaguely aware that a young man from Quinns had followed her. She was so deeply upset that she realised little of what went on around her, and stepped blindly off the pavement when the lights were red; a motor-cyclist pulled up with screeching brakes. The rider rasped:

"You silly bitch! You—" and then he saw her face, and broke off. He had been scared, but the sight of her expression drove fear away, as well as anger; the transformation was remarkable. A plump middle-aged man took Rebecca's arm with unwanted familiarity, and gave her a little squeeze.

"You really must be more careful, my dear. You need someone to look after you."

". . . dy jay walkers," contributed the driver of a passing car.

Rebecca tried to shake herself free, but the middle-aged man held firm.

"I'm sorry," she said. "I was—I wasn't thinking."

"But you should think, my dear," the middle-aged man insisted, and drew her a little closer. "Now why don't we go somewhere for a cup of tea, or to my club for a drink? It will give you time to recover."

"No, I—"

The motor-cyclist had pulled into the side of the road, and propped up his machine. He pushed through London's heedless, hurrying crowd, all rushing to cross before the lights changed again, and put a hand on the man's plump wrist.

"Okay, grandpa," he said. "You've done your good deed."

"Now, really—"

The motor-cyclist tightened his grip enough to make the middle-aged man wince, release Rebecca, mutter under his breath, and step into the road as the lights changed. For a moment, under the contemplative eye of a policeman on the other side of the road, Rebecca and the motor-cyclist stood together. The youth was of about the same height as the girl; stocky, fair-haired, freckled and fresh-looking. He had greeny-grey eyes.

"I didn't hurt you, did I?"

"Hurt—why, no," she said hurriedly. "No, I—I'd had some bad news, that's all. I'm all right. I'm sorry I've been a nuisance."

"You could walk around with your eyes shut all day without being a nuisance to me," declared the young man. "And I promise I shall never again call you a bitch." He smiled broadly; he had rather small and even teeth, and humour showed merry in his eyes. "How about coming and having that cuppa the old lecher suggested? You could hop on to the back of my bike, and I know a place not a thousand miles away which won't be crowded."

She looked at him seriously, for the first time. Until then he had been just someone standing near her, and she had been vaguely grateful because of the way he had dealt with the man with the clammy fingers; but now she saw him for a curly-haired youth of about her own age. And she felt so miserably unhappy, so running over with disappointment.

He took her arm with a grip very different from that of the middle-aged man.

"Take a chance," he urged. "I'm Terry McKay, with the purest mind of any man from County Mayo—and that was three generations back. The pillion's comfortable, guaranteed spring and sponge rubber." He glanced away from her to the constable, who had now crossed the road and was approaching. "I won't be a jiff," he said, apologetically. "I'm just making sure that I didn't hurt the young lady—I nearly ran her down."

"I noticed who nearly ran who down," the constable

said. He wasn't much older than the motor-cyclist, and looked rather envious. "Don't leave that death-trap in the kerb too long, will you?"

"We've got to hurry," Terry McKay urged Rebecca. "If the pillion isn't comfortable, give one scream and I'll let you get off."

Rebecca laughed. . . .

The policeman smiled.

Ten minutes later, the motor-cycle was parked in a narrow turning on the other side of Oxford Street, and Rebecca was sitting on a bamboo seat in front of a bamboo table, with wallpaper with a bamboo design and an occasional painted monkey all about her. At one end of the café, a glistening coffee-maker bubbled and grumbled, and an Italian girl with beautiful black eyes and a bouncy bosom sat reading *La Giornale.* There were only a few other customers. The motor-cyclist sat with his back to the window, Rebecca half-facing him, for he had selected a corner position.

A tall, black-haired young man with a soulful expression came towards them.

"They do marvellous pastries here," declared McKay. "Knock the French into the middle of next week. Like some?"

"Er—"

"Pastries, Luigi *mio*," ordered McKay. "And tea with mucho mucho hotta wotta."

"*Si*, signor," said Luigi, without a change in expression. He found his long-legged way back to the counter, while McKay leaned his elbows on the table, bent forward and looked into Rebecca's eyes. He studied her for so long that it was almost embarrassing, and then said:

"It's a crime."

"What's a crime?"

"A girl like you trying to commit suicide."

"Don't be absurd."

"So now I'm absurd?" He laughed at her. "I wish I knew how to work that miracle again."

She gave a funny kind of smile, puzzled and intrigued by him, still slightly embarrassed by the directness of his gaze, yet finding him wholly attractive.

"What miracle?"

"How to make you laugh."

"Laugh?" She frowned. "I don't remember—oh, I remember now!" She laughed again, and a moment later went on: "I didn't think I'd laugh for a long time."

"As a matter of fact, when I first noticed you, you looked as if you were going to burst into tears," declared McKay. "It doesn't take a great mind-reader to know that you've got plenty to worry about. Boss got fresh and fired you for noncooperation?"

She didn't comment.

"Boy-friend bowed out?" After a pause, McKay went on easily: "No, that can't be the answer, no human male would be such a fool." He gave her time to grasp what he meant, and went on again: "Of course you don't have to tell me your name or where you come from or what it's all about. It would be well-worth a dozen Italian cream pastries and imitation old English teas just to sit here for half an hour and look at you. How do you keep that complexion? *Is* it from bathing in milk?"

"Oh, you fool!"

"Granted," said McKay, and leaned back as the black-eyed girl came up with a plate of huge, gooey-looking cakes, the oozing cream from which was obviously fresh, and two large mugs of steaming tea. McKay offered Rebecca the cakes, took a large one himself, and scooped off some cream and jam. "Better than ever," he declared. "Now—"

Half an hour later, she had told him the story that she had told Mannering, as well as the facts which Mannering had told her. She had also eaten two mammoth cream cakes and finished a second mug of tea. Several other customers had come and gone, and the tiny dark-haired waitress was now reading a colourful woman's magazine.

Rebecca felt very much better, partly because she had

had time to absorb the situation, partly because it had been so easy to talk to Terry McKay. He had been a good listener, prompting her with the odd question here and there, but never showing the slightest inclination to take over or to guide the narrative. Now he sat with his back against the window, while the traffic outside built-up and became noisy with a kind of frenzied frustration, and people stamped or pattered along the pavement as if they dared not stop.

"So that's it," Terry remarked, heavily.

"I just don't know what to do," Rebecca said.

"This chap Mannering?"

"Yes."

"Could he be fooling you?"

"I don't think so for one minute."

"Be a bit late to think so if he's been pulling a fast one," said McKay drily. "If Sotheby's recommended him, he ought to be all right, but I've read some queer things about these Mayfair art and antique dealers. I think you ought to get another valuation of the jewels, you know. Where are they?"

"I left them with him—but he gave me a receipt," Rebecca replied hurriedly. He was beginning to alarm her, although she tried to reassure herself. She opened the shiny handbag. "Here it is, and here's the letter he gave me for my father, telling him it would take a few days and perhaps a week or more to get a true valuation."

"Could be just a stall," remarked McKay, musingly.

"But I asked him for it!"

"Yes, I remember," said McKay, and suddenly he closed his right hand over hers. "Becky, I'm sorry. I'm putting the wind up you more than ever, and there may be no cause for it. I wish you hadn't left the baubles with Mannering, though, then it would be easy to get another approximate valuation. I know—I once had to sell some old jewellery of my mother's, when we were on lean days, and it took the chap about thirty seconds." He glanced at a wrist watch. "It's nearly half-past five. Think it would be worth going back to the shop and asking him if you can have them back? That way you would be safe, wouldn't you?"

"It will look so odd," objected Rebecca.

McKay leaned further back in his seat, his eyes narrowed, his fingers drumming a tattoo on the bamboo table-top. It was warm in here, and his slightly snub nose and his forehead were shiny. As Rebecca watched him she began to feel even more uneasy, but suddenly his expression cleared.

"Got it!" he exclaimed.

"What have you got?"

"The answer to this little problem," declared McKay "I have a brother-in-law who works in the distribution department of the *Daily Globe*, and his sister is a girl friend of one of the chief reporters. Sit here a minute while I check on this Mannering!"

McKay's cool hand closed over Rebecca's again, as he slid out of his seat towards a telephone in a corner of the café. Left on her own, she was puzzled, a little alarmed, and very heavy-hearted again. She did not seriously doubt that Mannering's opinion was authentic, but there was now an edge of uncertainty; she hardly knew whether to be worried or hopeful about that. Pennies clanked into the prepayment call box, and she wondered whether McKay's brother-in-law would still be at his office. Then she thought of her father, waiting, so sure of himself, so patient, so content.

She bit her lips again.

.   .   .   .

Mannering was sitting in his office, thumbing through some old sale catalogues, and looking for items of jewellery which resembled the pieces which the girl had brought in. They had reminded him vaguely of jewels he had seen before, either at an exhibition, in a shop, or in a catalogue.

If he was right, and they had been sold at some auction

or offered for sale, it would be a little peculiar if they had been handed down by Rebecca Blest's relatives. His telephone bell rang as he flipped over the pages, and he lifted the receiver.

"Mannering."

"It's Tom, Mr. Mannering," announced Wainwright, the young assistant who had brought Rebecca to him. "A rather unexpected thing has happened, and I thought you ought to know at once."

"Go on, Tom."

"I followed the girl, and she nearly walked into a motor-cyclist," announced Tom. "They had a little heart-to-heart talk, and then she went off with him on the back of his bike. I wasn't near enough to hear what they said, but it looked like a pretty slick pick-up. On the other hand, it could have been prearranged. I managed to get a cab, and they're having tea in a café near Portman Square. The motor-cyclist is telephoning, and the girl's sitting on her own."

"How does she look?"

"Pretty fed-up."

"Stand by and see what happens next," ordered Mannering. "I shall be leaving here in about twenty minutes, and going straight home. Call me there if you think there's any need."

"Right, sir," said Tom. "If the affair fizzles out, I'll go home and report in the morning—will that be all right?"

"Yes," said Mannering.

He rang off, thumbed through more shiny pages without finding what he wanted, and then studied a note which he had made when the girl had been with him; a note about a Mr. Rett Larker, her uncle. Like the jewellery, the name rang a bell rather vaguely, and before long he lifted the telephone, dialled a Fleet Street number, and was answered promptly by a girl who announced:

"*Daily Globe.*"

"Is Mr. Chittering in, please?"

"Hold on," the girl said, and left him holding on for

several minutes, before he heard a man say casually: "Chittering here," in a disembodied-sounding voice. Then the voice became deeper. "Who's that? . . . Oh, John," went on Chittering, with an explosive laugh. "If it was anyone else I'd call it the long arm of coincidence, but as it's you I'll bet there's something sinister going on. One of our Distribution Department managers called me five minutes ago to find out if you were trustworthy and honest. Are you?"

"Use your own judgment," Mannering retorted. "What was it all about?"

"Some highly fanciful story about a sister-in-law or equally vague kind of relation wanting to check on your reliability on the valuation of old and venerable jools," declared Chittering, and Mannering's eyebrows shot up. "Breathe easy, I gave you a good reference. My conscience can answer for that in the next world. What can I do for you?"

"Does the name of Rett Larker mean anything to you?" inquired Mannering.

"Larker, Larker, there was Rhett Butler in *Gone With The Wind* . . . There's Sir James Larkin . . . There's . . . Did you say *Rett* Larker?"

"Yes."

"Not Larker—short 'a'. Lay-ker."

"She didn't spell the name, that could be it," said Mannering. "If you could stop being flippant for half a minute it would help."

"It's just my mood," said Chittering apologetically. "I'm trying to cheer myself up, but I think you may have managed to. Rett Laker was released from Her Majesty's Prison at Dartmoor about seven months ago, after serving fifteen years for murder, and having a life sentence commuted. That the chap you mean?"

3

DID THE LADY LIE?

"WELL, well," said Mannering, into the telephone. "And she didn't tell me."

"Who didn't tell you what?" demanded Chittering. "What's it all about, John? Another of your damsel in distress escapades? The more I know, the more I may be able to help."

"So you could," said Mannering, drily. "Yes. I'll keep in touch. Thanks." He rang off deliberately, hearing Chittering calling his name urgently; at that moment he did not want to have to concentrate on the newspaperman.

He sat back and pictured Rebecca Blest's face, especially her clear eyes, and told himself that it was difficult to believe that she had lied, even by implication. He recalled the jittery way she had spoken of her uncle, and her tense: "It's almost as if he had stretched out from the grave to hurt my father." Grave, not prison. Had she passed over the fact that Uncle Rett had spent a long time in prison because of embarrassment, or family pride, or shame? When she had learned that the jewels were faked, wasn't her normal reaction likely to be that an ex-jail bird uncle knew something about it—and in the kind of mood any honest girl would have been in, wouldn't she have confided in him?

"I'd like to find out," Mannering said in a thoughtful voice, and then the telephone bell rang on his desk. Was it Chittering, trying again? Fleet Street bred a race of men who never gave up. He heard Larraby, his manager, speak on the extension, and a moment later there was a tap at the door.

"It's Mrs. Mannering, sir."

"Oh, thanks," said Mannering, and picked up the

receiver as Larraby's grey head disappeared from the doorway. A warm note came into his voice. "Hallo, darling. If this is to inquire why I'm not home, I'm nearly on my way."

"It's to explain why I'm not home," said Lorna Mannering. "John—"

"Hmm?"

"Could you stand an evening on your own?"

"Oh, I should think so," said Mannering airily. "I haven't been to the Soho Strip area for a few weeks, and—"

"You stay away from Soho strips and strippers unless you take me with you," Lorna ordered. "Darling, Meg Ustley wants me to do a portrait of her seven-year-olds, and to talk about it over dinner. I think she might be able to persuade me."

"You go and be persuaded," Mannering encouraged. "I'll eat at the club, and—"

"Ethel's home, and she'll have dinner ready," Lorna said. "I'll call and tell her that I won't be in. Must rush, darling—'bye."

Mannering said: "Stipulate a big fat fee"—and rang off much more slowly than he had from Chittering.

He glanced up at Lorna's portrait of him, feeling mild pleasure at the fact that she had found a subject which she was eager to paint, and then thought of Rebecca Blest as she might be if Lorna put her on canvas. *Very* beautiful, with a touch of Millais of the *Bubbles* era. *Pretty?* It wasn't exactly the word. *Simple?* Was she so simple, if she had lied even by implication?

He glanced at his notes, and saw her address next to the name of Samuel Blest. If Blest were a true name, then Rett Laker was her mother's brother; Mannering was never very good at working out other people's family trees, and wasn't quite sure where that came in. He memorised the address: *127, Mapperley Street, Notting Hill.* But for Lorna's telephone call he would not have thought of going there, but the news from Chittering had piqued him, and if he appeared on the doorstep, he might startle the girl into telling the whole truth. It was now half-past six; he could be at Notting Hill by half-past seven, and back at his flat by eight, for dinner.

He locked his desk, went out, and saw Larraby getting up from a long desk-like counter behind the shop. From here he could see the whole length of the shop itself, but could not be seen from the window or from the front door.

"Time you went home, Josh," Mannering said.

"I'm in no hurry," said Larraby. "Shall I lock up?"

"Will you?" asked Mannering, and as an afterthought he added: "I'm going to see the girl Blest. I think she might be trying to dangle me on a piece of string."

"I didn't get that impression," said Larraby.

Mannering smiled. "Nor did Tom!"

He left Larraby to the 'locking-up'; which meant switching on the current which was the first defence against burglars, and putting the electronic devices, the second defence, on *Active*. As he moved away from Larraby, he heard a woman's voice:

"Darling, that's absolutely *beautiful*."

The depth of feeling, almost of emotion, could not be mistaken. The electric relay system carried conversation from outside the window into the shop, for thieves had been known to confide in accomplices just before making a raid, and many had been thwarted without knowing that their plotting could be overheard.

Mannering saw a couple standing at the narrow window, looking at the single diamond watch which lay there against a background of black velvet. The watch had been made for an ill-fated Queen of France, and was now nearly priceless, although some collector would probably buy it and lock it away so that he could gloat over his riches and his rarities.

". . . I've never seen anything like it," the woman was saying.

Mannering stepped out into Hart Row. The man glanced at him; heavily-built, well-dressed, wearing a curly-brimmed bowler hat. He gave Mannering a rueful half-smile; his wife was absorbed in the watch.

". . . I can't guess how much it would be," she said, almost sighing.

Mannering murmured: "When it was sold at Christie's seven years ago, the reserve price was twenty-one thousand pounds."

"Twenty-one *thousand*!" The woman spun round.

"I'll have two of them," said her husband, airily. "One for each wrist."

Mannering touched his hat to the woman, and went on, annoyed by the man's flippancy although he had no good cause to be; but a watch like that, any genuine antique or really old jewellery, any *objet d'art*, was a thing to reverence, not to joke about. He was wondering rather wryly: "how pompous can one get?" as he walked along to his car. It was parked at the end of Hart Row, at a small site which would soon be built on, so giving him a parking problem. The car, a silver grey Bristol, was being admired by two youngsters, who backed away hurriedly as he approached.

As he eased his way through the dwindling traffic of the West End, Mannering contrasted his own circumstances with those of Rebecca Blest, for instance. Money in moderate amounts hardly affected him or Lorna, and in recent years profits from Quinns had risen sharply, although his accountant frequently told him that he could safely charge more than he did. That girl had believed that she was in sight of a fortune, and had been so terribly disappointed.

Mannering could not tell himself why he was anxious to find out whether she had known that Uncle Rett Laker had been a jail bird or not. If he had to give a reason, he would probably say that it was to find out whether a pair of pretty eyes had fooled him; he had felt so sure that the girl was absolutely honest.

At two minutes to seven, he turned into Mapperley Street. This was near the main road, and the houses on either side were of four storeys. A few plane trees bordered the pavement. A few houses were newly painted. Many of them had several bell pushes in the front porch, showing that they had been turned into flats. He stopped near number 100, got out, and strolled towards 127. The first thing which caught his eye was a motor-cycle propped up outside the front door. Was it the motor-cyclist of whom Tom had talked? If so, had that been a chance meeting, or one by arrangement?

He found the street door ajar. A little name plate said:
"*H. Ashton—Ground Floor.*"
"*S. Blest—1st Floor.*"
He went into a gloomy hall and up a flight of narrow steps to the first floor, and as he did so, he heard a woman crying.

. . . . .

Rebecca Blest did not think she would ever understand why she had been willing to let Terry McKay take her on the pillion of his motor-cycle, but when she reached the street door of her home, about half-past seven that evening, she knew that she was very glad Terry was there. She disliked the thought of going to talk to her father, hated the thought of disappointing him, felt that without the stranger, she would have been utterly alone. When he had come from the telephone, cheerfully reassuring her about Mannering, she had felt relieved and free from the deepest anxiety—that she and her father were being cheated.

"According to my brudder-in-law, this Mannering is quite a guy," McKay had assured her. "Even the great men at Scotland Yard consult him about jewels sometimes. It looks as if you're in the safest of safe hands, what with Mannering and me! Not looking forward to telling your old Dad, are you?"

"Not a bit."

"Tell you what, let me give you some moral support."

Terry had said. "I needn't come in, I can stall around, and if you need a shoulder to weep on, it will be there. How about that?"

"No, you've been too good already—"

"Woosh!" Terry McKay had said, and put a hand at her elbow, hoisted her to her feet, paid the bill, boomed a cheerful good night to Luigi, and led the way outside. He had ridden to Notting Hill very carefully, as if to make sure that Rebecca had no possible cause for alarm, and just before seven they had reached the street.

"And I shall stay here until you come down to give me marching orders," McKay had declared. "I'm not hungry, take your time!" He had watched her go into the house, noticing that the street door was unlocked, and then he had walked up and down Mapperley Street, glancing up at the window of her flat occasionally, quite prepared to wait for hours . . .

Rebecca went upstairs.

The familiar gloomy staircase seemed to be more than ever full of shadows and blackness tonight, although she knew that it was because of her mood. This was the worst moment—between closing the street door, and opening the front door of the three-roomed flat. Her footsteps dragged until, near the landing, she made herself put on a spurt, and reached the front door briskly. She took out her key, still moving quickly, fumbled for the keyhole in the poor light, and then dropped the key. "Little fool!" she snapped at herself, and bent down to grope for it. She picked it up, took a firmer hold, and tried again. This time she found the keyhole at the first attempt. She turned the key, drew a deep breath, and thrust the door open; then called out, in a cheerful-sounding voice:

"I'm back, Dad!"

Her father did not answer.

"Hey, there!" she called again. "I'm back!" She closed the door behind her, and, forcing gaiety, went hurrying into the big front room, overlooking the street—the living-room and dining-room, the general purpose room, with the telephone, the old furniture, the old carpets, most of which she could remember from her childhood.

There was still no answer.

"Dad, where are you?" she called.

She was already puzzled, but not yet worried; usually her father would call "Half a jiff!" even if he were in the bathroom. She turned towards the rooms on the other side of the narrow passage, and saw that the bathroom door was ajar, but there was no sign of movement. *He must have gone out*, she told herself, but was even more puzzled because tonight of all nights she had expected him to be in, waiting—waiting so eagerly. She shouldn't have stayed out so long with Terry; she had only herself to blame. With so much at stake, her father must have been beside himself with anxiety.

"Dad!" she called.

She heard nothing, but noticed that his bedroom door was closed. She hesitated, just outside it. He might have been taken ill, of course—it was quite possible that the delay and the anxiety had affected him so that his heart had played him up again. She still hesitated, now afraid of what she might find, then suddenly grasped the handle of the door firmly, and thrust the door open.

"Father, are you all right?"

He was there, but did not answer. She saw his feet at the foot of the bed. The head of the bed was behind the door, to keep him out of draughts; the window was on one side.

She hurried further in, anxiety sharpening her voice: "Father, are you—?"

She stopped half-way to the bed, staring round and down at him, so dreadfully shocked that she could not move. In fact, she could hardly breathe, for what had happened was so terrible.

He lay on his side, He was fully clad. Someone had smashed heavy blows on his balding head, so that there was only blood and horror.

Rebecca felt her senses swimming. She felt nausea,

which suddenly affected her whole body, and she began to tremble. She backed away, clutching at the door for support, and then suddenly turned her head away, so that she could not see, and buried her face against her arm.

She began to struggle for breath; apart from the sounds she made, there was only an awful silence.

4

WHY MURDER?

MANNERING stood outside the door and heard the girl crying; frowned, and hesitated before ringing the bell or knocking. He listened for other sounds, and thought that he heard a man making soothing noises, but was not sure. He stood quite still. From the flat below the sound of music came suddenly, as someone switched on radio or television, and a car passed noisily in the street. After this, he heard a man's voice from the other side of the door.

"We mustn't wait any longer, Becky. We've got to send for the police."

The girl seemed to be trying to stifle her sobs.

Mannering thought: *Police?* and rapped sharply on the door with his knuckles. Man and girl broke off, and it seemed a long time before the girl asked, in a scared voice:

"Who's that?"

"Soon see," said the man, and Mannering heard footsteps before the door opened. A thickset young man of medium height stood there, freckled, curly-haired—almost certainly Tom's motor-cyclist; he wore a black windcheater of plastic or leather, and a pair of thick gloves dangled from a webbing belt round his waist. Out of sight, the girl called:

"Who is it?"

"It's John Mannering, Miss Blest," Mannering announced.

"What the heck are you doing here?" the motor-cyclist demanded, and added quickly: "Changed your mind about those jewels?"

"What's the trouble here?" Mannering inquired, and the young man stood aside to allow him to pass. The girl was standing in the open doorway of a room on the right;

beyond her, Mannering could just see a television set, and a window overlooking the street. All prettiness had been wiped away with tears. Her eyes were swollen, her cheeks smeared, even her hair bedraggled. She had a shocked look, too; Mannering had seen shock too often to be in any doubt of that.

"What *is* the trouble?" he demanded.

The girl said: "My—my father—" and then swung round with her hand at her lips, as if she were biting her fingers to prevent herself from bursting into tears. The motor-cyclist was pale, too; a look in his eyes suggested to Mannering that he was doing his best to put up a bold front, but didn't feel too good.

"Her father's dead," he muttered. "He's—dead."

"Did the shock kill him?" Mannering asked, and for the first time allowed himself to wonder if there could be the slightest doubt about the value of the jewellery. In that moment, he took it for granted that Blest had died when he had been told the truth; it wasn't until the motor-cyclist said gruffly: "No—it wasn't shock," that he began to think beyond the obvious possibility. Without another word the youth led him towards another door, and into a bedroom.

Then Mannering saw exactly what the girl had seen.

He stood very still. The motor-cyclist was looking away from the battered head, and towards the window, as if he could not bear the sight any longer. There was silence in the flat; only the noise of traffic in the street made any sound. Mannering glanced about the room, seeing that everything was tidy. There was no indication that the wardrobe, the chest of drawers or anything here had been searched.

"You were quite right, it's time you went for the police," he said. "I saw a telephone kiosk at the corner. Have you any change for it?"

"Yes."

"Don't ring 999," advised Mannering. "Dial Whitehall 1212 and ask for Superintendent Bristow. If he's in, tell him that I'm here, will you? And tell his personal assistant, if he's not there."

The youth said: "Yes, all right," and turned out of the bedroom, but he didn't go far away. "You'll look after her?"

"Yes."

"Why did you come here?"

"We can talk about that later," said Mannering. "You can tell me what happened when you picked Rebecca up in Bond Street, too." He waited for the glint of surprise in the grey-green eyes, and then pushed past the youth towards the front room.

The girl was standing near a window, staring across the road, one hand at her lips. The front door opened and closed. The girl turned slowly and looked hurtfully into Mannering's eyes, then moved to a chair and lowered herself to the arm. Still staring at him, she said:

"That was how I found him. I thought he—he had had a heart attack. He didn't answer when I called out, so I went to his room and saw his legs, and then I looked round the door, and I saw—oh, God! Why did they have to do that to him? Why did they have to do it? Who would want to hurt a dear old man like that?"

The words came almost incoherently, and there were long pauses between some of them.

Mannering said: "There's one good thing; he didn't suffer."

"How do you know he didn't suffer?" she blazed up at him. "How can you possibly know— ?"

"Rebecca—"

"How can anybody know? It was awful, it—"

"He didn't suffer," Mannering said sharply, and Rebecca broke off, as if beginning to wonder whether he really did know what he was talking about. "He must have been lying on his side, asleep," Mannering explained. "His arms and legs are in a perfectly natural position. That was the first thing I noticed. Whoever did it got into the flat without waking him, stood over him, and struck without waking him, too. I doubt whether he knew what was happening—it couldn't have happened more quickly."

Her eyes looked huge.

"You're not—you're not just saying this?"

"In a little while, a Home Office pathologist will be here, and I'm positive that he will tell you exactly the same thing," said Mannering. "There isn't any doubt about how it happened. And it means that your father didn't live to learn the truth about the jewellery. Did he often take a nap in the afternoons?"

"Yes," Rebecca said, and squeezed her eyes tightly, and moistened her lips. "Yes, always, the doctor said—" She broke off, raised her hands to her breast, and cried out in a shrill voice: "But who would do such a thing? Who would want to kill him?"

"That's what we have to find out," Mannering said. "Rebecca, the police are going to ask a lot of questions. They can't help the fact that you feel shocked and grief-stricken. Their job is to get as much information out of you as they can before a doctor gives you a sedative and helps you to rest. Then—"

"*Rest!*"

"You'll have to rest," Mannering told her gently. "And I'm saying all this because I think you ought to tell the police everything you possibly can, and as quickly as you can."

She didn't answer.

"Understand me, Rebecca?"

She was biting her lips. "Of course I'll tell them," she said, suddenly shrill. "I'll do anything to help them catch this devil."

"Then tell them what you forgot to tell me," said Mannering, and he touched her arm. "Keeping it from me didn't matter at all, but half truths and evasions with the police always lead to difficulties."

After a pause, Rebecca said: "I don't understand you. Half truths about what?"

"Your Uncle Rett Laker."

"*Half* truths?"

"Evasions then," corrected Mannering. He was glad that he had managed to make the girl think about something more than the hideous truth. It would do no harm if she were annoyed with him, even angry with him. It was essential that something should break through the awful numbness of her grief, and that she should be able to face the police fairly calmly. "You didn't tell me that your Uncle Rett had spent the last fifteen years in prison. The police—"

She cried: "What?"

That was the first moment when Mannering had any doubt that she knew; until then he had taken it for granted that shame had kept her quiet, but now he thought, startled: *She's really surprised.* He studied her as she took a step nearer, reading the bewilderment on her face.

"Your uncle spent the last fifteen years in prison," Mannering said. "When I discovered that, I came to see you."

"But I don't believe it!"

"You didn't seem to have much love for him," said Mannering; and then another, very simple possibility occurred to him: that Chittering had told him of a different man, that the Rett Larker he had talked about wasn't this girl's uncle. Larker or *Laker*? "How do you spell Larker?"

"LAKER," she answered.

"How often did you see him?"

She didn't answer. A car came along the road very fast, then began to slow down: Mannering had no doubt that it was a police car. He didn't look out of the window, but concentrated on Rebecca, especially on this new, startled expression in her eyes; it was almost as if the truth were slowly dawning on her.

"How often?" he urged.

"I—I saw him frequently when I was very young,"

she said. "Before he went away to—to Australia." She caught her breath. Outside, a car door slammed. "Then I didn't see him for years—until a few months ago. I hated the sight of him then, he—he was sarcastic with my father. And they kept quarrelling. I don't know what they quarrelled about, but it was something which went pretty deep. You mean—he *was* in prison."

"He was in prison," Mannering assured her.

There was a tap at the door as he spoke. Mannering opened it, to see a little grey-haired woman and a biggish, thickset middle-aged man, standing outside.

"Now what's going on here?" the man demanded. "We live downstairs, and we heard Becky crying and a lot of people walking about—"

"Becky!" cried the woman, as Rebecca appeared at the room doorway.

They all went in.

"What is it? What's the matter?" demanded the woman. "What's upset you so?"

"It's terrible, Mrs. Ashton," Rebecca Blest managed to say. "My—my father—"

"All right," Mannering said. "I'll tell them, Rebecca, a little later, I think the police are here."

Footsteps were sounding in the house, heavy but un-hurried, as the police were likely to come if there was need for them but no emergency. The girl looked astoun-ded, the man and woman seemed shocked. Then men sounded at the head of the stairs, and one asked briskly:

"Where are they?"

"In there, I think," said the motor-cyclist.

"And you say your name is Terence McKay, and that you hadn't met Miss Blest until today."

"I'm McKay, and I met Becky Blest this afternoon—about five o'clock, I suppose," said the motor-cyclist.

The door opened, and a uniformed sergeant came in with the youth. The sergeant was a middle-aged man with a thick grey close-trimmed moustache; he filled his uni-form too tightly. He wore a peaked cap, and had obviously come from a patrol car. He had very pale blue eyes, and a clear, fresh complexion.

"Miss Rebecca Blest?"

"Yes," Rebecca answered.

"I'm very sorry to hear what's happened, Miss Blest," the sergeant said. "In a few minutes the officer in charge of investigations will be here. Until then, I think you'd better take it easy." He was setting out to win her confidence, Mannering noticed almost with amusement— but amusement couldn't be very close with that body in the room across the passage. "Is there anything you want?"

"No—no thank you."

"We've just come up from our flat. We'll be there if we're wanted," the man Ashton said, and moved towards the door. His wife followed. The sergeant asked their names, then let them go.

"Are you a friend of the young lady, sir?" the sergeant asked Mannering, when the Ashtons had gone.

"A business acquaintance," Mannering said. The pale blue eyes appeared to be studying him speculatively; suddenly recognition dawned, and the man's face lit up; it made him seem ten years younger.

"You're Mr. John Mannering!"

"Yes, sergeant."

"Well, I'm—" he began; then appeared to realise that he wasn't being correct enough, and stiffened. "I'll be glad if you will refrain from asking the young lady questions," he said. "The Divisional Chief Inspector is on his way."

"Who is he?" inquired Mannering.

"Mr. Ingleby, sir."

Mannering thought: Well, I have some of the luck.

Ingleby had been at the Yard until a few years ago, and transferred to the Division at his own request on compassionate grounds—he had an ailing wife who could not move out of her home very much by herself. Ingleby would be a good man to work with. As the thought entered his head, Mannering realised wryly that he was taking it for granted that he would become deeply involved. He was not sure that he relished the idea, and was positive that his wife wouldn't. But there were too many unanswered questions—the mystery of fake jewels which should have been real but were false; the mystery of Rett Laker; the mystery of this cold-blooded killing. There were other puzzles, too: was this clear-eyed, apparently pleasant young man really a stranger caught up in a thick web of crime? Or had he been watching out for Rebecca, and deliberately scraped an acquaintance?

He heard another car pulling up outside.

"Rebecca," he said quietly, "my advice remains exactly the same—tell the police everything you know." He saw the sergeant nod ponderously, as he went into the passage. A uniformed constable stood outside the door of the room where the old man lay dead; he stiffened to attention when Mannering appeared. Footsteps sounded on the stairs, and a man spoke briskly:

"Nothing's been touched, and no one's left the premises, have they?" That was the incisive voice of Claude Ingleby.

"No, sir," an unseen man assured him.

"Good," Ingleby said, and came in. He caught sight of Mannering, and stopped short. Mannering smiled at him, confident of a friendly if surprised greeting. He was not prepared for the way Ingleby began to frown, the way the man stared at him as if at a stranger; or at least as if at someone whom he did not particularly like.

5

SHARP POLICEMAN

"What are you doing here?" demanded Ingleby.

"That's a long story," Mannering said, still smiling.

"It had better be a good one," Ingleby said acidly. "Wait, please." He saw the uniformed sergeant come out of the big room, and without a pause, he asked: "Is there a room where Mr. Mannering and the youth McKay can wait?"

"There's the kitchen, sir, or the young lady's bedroom," the sergeant replied. He glanced at Mannering as if he also was puzzled by the reception.

Inside the big room, McKay murmured something to Rebecca which Mannering could not catch.

"We'll use the kitchen," Ingleby said. "Mr. Mannering, will you please wait?"

"For how long?" inquired Mannering, no longer smiling.

"For as long as it takes me to complete the initial stages of my inquiry."

Mannering stared at the detective, sensing deep antagonism, wishing that he had even an inkling of the reason for it. Seconds seemed to pass very quickly. It was some time since he had come into conflict with a hostile policeman, but it had happened often enough in the past, and in the past his reaction had always been the same: to be as difficult with the police as they were with him.

"Sorry," he said brusquely. "I haven't time."

"Then you must make time."

Mannering said: "Chief Inspector, I shall be at my flat in Green Street, Chelsea from nine o'clock onward, and will be glad to answer any questions if you care to come there." He waited long enough to challenge Ingleby's angry gaze, then pushed past the man towards the door. Two policemen were between him and the door, and would try to stop him at a word or a nod from Ingleby. This was a moment of decision, in its way—a testing time. If Ingleby's manner was dictated from a position of strength, he would exert himself to keep his witness here.

Ingleby called: "Mannering!"

Mannering turned to look at him.

"Yes?"

"You ought to know better than to act in defiance of the police."

"Yes, oughtn't I?" said Mannering. "This is a night when a lot of people ought to know better. There's one thing you might remember, Chief Inspector—a man is lying dead in there, and his daughter needs time and help to recover from the shock." He nodded curtly, turned away, and stepped past the dead man's room, then on to the landing outside; neither of the policemen attempted to stop him, so Ingleby had given no silent instruction. There was a chance that men on duty in the street would try to stop him, but none of them did.

Ashton was coming out of his front door, carrying an empty coal bucket. Mannering nodded, and walked towards his car, reflecting that Ingleby might have recognised it as his and then decided that it was unlikely; the Bristol was comparatively new. He took the wheel, his mind filled with an uneasy confusion of thoughts. He would have liked to help the girl more; in a queer way, he felt that he was letting her down. But he would not have been much help to her cooped up in the kitchen. There were so many things to think about, but the one which nagged at him most was Ingleby's manner. As he turned towards the West End, he said aloud:

"He wouldn't put on that act without a reason."

What reason could there be?

Mannering reached Green Street, Chelsea, which opened on to the Embankment at the south end, and

drove along slowly, wondering whether the police had
carried their hostility to the stage of stationing men in
the street to watch him. He saw none. He pulled up outside the house where he had his flat, knowing that he
would probably have to go out again this evening. As he
went upstairs in the small, recently installed lift, he
wished that Lorna were in; he could talk about this to
her, instead of eating a solitary meal. At least he was
hungry; nothing had put him off his food, and he had had
a light lunch.

He let himself in with his key, and there was a faint
aroma of roasting chicken; left on her own Ethel the cook-
cum-maid always fell back on chicken, and she cooked it
perfectly. Mannering went to the kitchen, put his head
round the door, saw her bending over the oven door, and
said: "Mind it doesn't bite you." He smiled as she started,
and twisted her head round. "How long have I got?" he
inquired.

"Well, sir, you're late already. I can't help it if it's a
bit overdone, I can't really."

"No bath, then," said Mannering. "Ten minutes?"

"You won't be any longer, sir, will you?" Ethel was a
tall, thin, worried-looking girl, flustered and too hot.

"Not a minute longer," Mannering assured her. He
went into his bedroom, washed at the handbasin, and
shrugged himself into a light-weight jacket, looser fitting
than the one he had worn during the day. He went into
the dining-room, poured himself a whisky and soda, and
was sipping it when Ethel came in. Twenty minutes later,
he finished an apple fool cooked as with an angel's hand,
feeling as replete as one could be.

He was only vaguely aware that he ought to be much
more worried—if not about Ingleby's manner, then about
Rebecca Blest. He went into his small study, sat down by
the window, resisted the temptation to switch on television, and began to go over the events of the afternoon
one by one. Soon afterwards he began to write down in
its proper sequence everything that had happened.

He wished Tom would ring up—Tom could give him more information about the encounter between Rebecca and the motor-cyclist.

The telephone bell rang.

He had been half waiting for that since he had come in, and hitched his chair nearer so that he could lift the receiver without getting up. It was an even bet between the police, young McKay and the newspapers, he decided; and on the whole the thought of McKay was the most likely.

A man asked: "Is Mr. Mannering there?"

"Yes, speaking," Mannering answered, sure that the voice was unfamiliar.

"Very glad to have the opportunity of speaking to you, Mr. Mannering," the caller said; there was a slightly obsequious note in his voice, giving the impression that he was a man whom it would be easy to dislike on sight. "I've got a little business proposition I would like to put to you, but it's very confidential. Are you free this evening?"

"I could be," Mannering said cautiously.

"Always free if you can make a pound or so, eh?" There was a cackle of a laugh at the end of the 'eh', and Mannering now wondered if the man was nervous. "Well, you'll make plenty out of this, there's no doubt about that. Could you meet me at the statue of Achilles in Hyde Park in an hour's time, say?"

"No, I could not."

"Now, Mr. Mannering—"

"I said no and I meant no," Mannering insisted, and tried to prevent himself from speaking too brusquely. "I could see you here, if you're sure that it's worth while."

"Oh, it's worth while," the man assured him, and that cackle of laughter came again. "But I don't want to come to your place."

"That's too bad," Mannering said. "I have to stay at home. Good night."

The man cried: "Mannering! Don't ring off."

Mannering said: "I can't think why I shouldn't. You haven't told me who you are, why you got in touch with me, and what it's all about."

There was a pause, which became so prolonged that Mannering wondered if the man had silently rung off, and gone away. Then he heard the distant sound of a car engine, and knew that the line was still open. He was intrigued, and still waited; but it would not be long before he was annoyed. There was enough on his mind without this. At the back of his mind, indeed, there was the possibility that this call had something to do with what had happened earlier in the day—it was almost too much to believe that there would be two separate new mysteries in the space of a few hours.

"Are you there?" he asked at last.

"Listen to me, Mr. Mannering," the man urged. "This is big money. It's really big. You're the best man in the country to handle it, because you've got just the right outlet at Quinns. I'll tell you one thing, for a start—if you want to put your hands on the genuine jewellery that Rebecca Blest thought she had this afternoon, I can put you on to it. That *and* a lot more. But you've got to take a chance. You can't make a fortune without some risk."

Mannering said: "I'm not coming out tonight, but I'll be at home all the evening."

"Mannering! I tell you—"

Mannering said: "Good night," and rang off.

The moment he had cut the line he had misgivings, but he told himself that the man would try again if he were really serious; there was no reason at all to believe that he wasn't. The hunch that this had something to do with the girl's visit seemed now to have had a kind of inevitability.

He moved from the telephone, lit a cigarette, and tried to interest himself in *The Times*, but every news item and every article palled. He wondered whether he was more edgy than the circumstances warranted, whether he wasn't making mistakes. This was the third time within the course of a few hours when he had cut an interview or a conversation short—first Chittering, then Ingleby, now this unknown man. It was one thing to persuade himself that the man would not give up after one call, but supposing he did?

The telephone bell rang again.

"Ah," said Mannering, with satisfaction, and began to wonder what kind of a rendezvous he could make with the cackler. For the moment he did not want the police to know about it; if the police were near the meeting place, any criminal would realise it, and would also realise that he was on the spot. Chittering might be glad to help—or young Tom, or one of the other younger members of the staff. He lifted the telephone. "John Mannering here."

"Hold on, please," a man said. "Chief Inspector Ingleby wants you."

"Oh," said Mannering, acutely disappointed. He sat back in his chair, waiting, beginning to frown as the telephone was silent for so long. Then Ingleby came on briskly.

"Mr. Mannering?"

"Yes."

"Sorry to keep you. Will you be in if I come to see you right away?"

"Yes."

"Thanks," said Ingleby. "Say in half an hour."

He rang off without another word. Mannering put his receiver down, looked up at the ceiling, and smiled uneasily; he was really being hoist with his own petard, and wasn't sure that he could blame the policeman. Another question came into his mind: *why had Ingleby called from the Division?* Usually the Yard dealt with him, Mannering, whenever there was need, and he could not recall a visit from a Divisional officer for a long time. Hadn't Ingleby consulted the Yard? The question itself was almost superfluous; Mannering could be sure that no London C.I.D. man could take this kind of step without having the Yard's approval. It added still more to the puzzle.

He called the *Globe*, but Chittering was out.

He called young Tom Wainwright, whose mother answered; Tom was out with a girl friend.

He put a call to Larraby's small flat, a one-room and bathroom apartment not far from Quinns; Larraby liked living in bachelor freedom, and also liked being within easy walking distance of his work. The telephone rang on and on, until Mannering remembered that a few days ago his manager had told him that he was going to Covent Garden tonight, for some special charity opera. Mannering rang off, frustrated. A quarter of an hour had already passed since Ingleby had telephoned, so there wasn't long for the mystery man to call back, and it was beginning to look as if he had made a mistake about that. Well, he could blame no one but himself.

He waited for another ten minutes, smoking more vigorously than he usually did, restless, edgy. Ethel looked in. Was it all right if she went out for an hour? She had promised to go and see a friend. Mannering heard the front door close on her. There could be no more than five minutes before Ingleby was due. This seemed a night when everyone was determined to desert him. He laughed at the thought, and the front door bell broke across his laughter.

"Well, he's prompt," he said aloud, and stubbed out a cigarette and went into the hall. If it were possible to make peace, he intended to make it; there was no point in being on bad terms with the police, and it would be much better to confide in them.

He opened the front door.

A man, a stranger, stood leaning against the wall at one side. He had his right hand up against his forehead, the fingers spread-eagled, and through the fingers Mannering could see the crimson of blood on fair hair. There was a splash of crimson on the man's flabby cheeks, too. His eyes looked glassy. He tried to form words but could hardly make a sound; Mannering thought that he was trying to say: "*Mannering.*"

Mannering said quickly:

"All right, I'll look after you," and kicked the door wider open, then stepped to the side of the injured man. It was impossible to judge how badly he was hurt, but could he have got this far if the injury were really serious? He kept his hand at his head as Mannering put an arm round his waist and helped him into and across the flat, to the bathroom. He pushed that door open, guided the man to a stool, and helped him to sit down. He could hear the other's whistling breath; the man was almost a dead weight, he had been able only to shuffle along. Mannering propped him up against the wall, and said:

"I'll telephone for a doctor. I won't be a jiff." He hurried out of the bathroom with a picture of Rebecca Blest's father's head in his mind's eye; Blest had been killed by just such a blow as this.

He was dialling his own doctor's number when the front door bell rang. This time, it was Ingleby.

6

CAUSE FOR SUSPICION

HALF an hour later, Mannering's doctor and the local police-surgeon left the flat in the wake of the ambulance men, who had just carried the injured man out of the hall. By the time the first doctor had arrived the man had been unconscious; and if medical opinion were vindicated, he was not likely to live through the night. Mannering could almost hear the doctor saying, as if to himself:

"Can't understand how he got up here—just can't understand it."

Ingleby had said very little, but had called the local police-surgeon, talked to the Yard and to the Division, and been briskly efficient. The hostility still existed, Mannering knew, although it was subdued. Ingleby had come by himself, which could be construed as a friendly gesture, but other C.I.D. men had since arrived. The familiar process of searching for clues, checking the polished boards and the rugs on them for blood stains, checking the landing outside for the same things, had gone on while the doctors had been examining the injured man.

Now Ingleby was downstairs with the C.I.D. man, and for a few minutes Mannering was alone in the flat. It was nearly ten o'clock. He wondered what time Lorna would be home, and toyed with the idea of telephoning and warning her what to expect; but before he went to the telephone, Ingleby came in through the partly open door.

"Has he gone?" Mannering asked.

"Just been driven off," said Ingleby. "Anxious about him?"

"I'd like to think he would live to talk."

Ingleby asked: "Would you?"

The question was like the drip of iced water; cold and

47

stinging. An ominous significance was hidden there. Mannering studied Ingleby as he stood with his back to the open door, stern-faced and hard-eyed; his hostility was as real as ever.

Mannering said: "I don't know what's on your mind, but I can't say I like the way it makes you behave. Come into the study, and have a drink."

In the study, Ingleby said: "I won't drink, thank you." He sat rather stiffly in a William and Mary slung chair which had been darkened by years of polishing and use until it was almost black, while Mannering sat in a chair covered with wine-red mohair.

"Please yourself," said Mannering. "Yes, I would."

"Would what?"

"Like to think that chap will live to talk." When Ingleby didn't respond, Mannering fought back a wave of irritability. "Supposing you tell me what's on your mind, Ingleby? Then I might be able to get it off."

Ingleby said: "Mr. Mannering, there are no bloodstains on the floor of the hall downstairs. There are none on the pavement, as far as my men have been able to discover—they're getting special lights, to check by, and they'll be reporting very soon. But at the moment there is nothing but your evidence to say that the man was injured when he arrived. There are not even any bloodstains or indications that he leaned against the wall outside the door. There are one or two spots of blood on the floor in here—there were, rather, before my men scraped them up, to test for the blood group. But anything found inside the flat would hardly help to corroborate your statement, would it?"

Mannering stared at him, his heart beginning to pound.

"No doubt you see the obvious implication," Ingleby said.

After a pause, Mannering replied: "Oh, yes, I can see, the implication—that he wasn't attacked outside at all, but was attacked in here."

"Precisely."

"By me?"

"No one else was here when I arrived, and you told me that no one else had been here this evening, except your maid." Ingleby paused, and then added acidly: "She has conveniently gone out."

"Very conveniently," Mannering agreed heavily. This wasn't the moment to say that Ethel had gone at her own request, but the time might come when it would be invaluable for her to say so. "So your guess is that this man came to see me here and that I hit him over the head."

"I didn't say that."

"Didn't you?" murmured Mannering. He resisted a temptation to get up and move about; that would make it look as if he were too much on edge. "And Rebecca Blest's father was killed in the same way and with the same kind of weapon. Do you think I did that too?"

Ingleby didn't answer.

"Now if you could only find the weapon—" Mannering began. "And if you could only find my fingerprints on it, then you really would have a case."

Ingleby stared at him gravely for a long time; for so long and so intently that his gaze was disquieting. Mannering put his hand to his pocket for cigarettes, and took it away again. It was difficult not to look away from the C.I.D. man, but one or the other of them would have to, first. It was like playing the silly children's game of staring-you-out. His own gaze was about to shift when Ingleby turned away for a moment, then looked back, and said crisply:

"We have found the weapon."

"*What?*"

"We have found the weapon, Mr. Mannering."

"Don't be absurd. It's not here."

"It was here."

Mannering thought: I'm going crazy. Ingleby wouldn't make a flat statement like that unless he was sure of himself, yet on the face of it, this looked like nonsense. There was one way to force the issue, and he used it.

"I don't believe it."

"There are three witnesses," Ingleby declared. He opened his case, delved a hand inside, and brought out a short-handled hammer with a heavy iron head, daubed thick with blood and with hairs sticking to the blood. The handle was smeared with grey powder, and seemed to be quite clear of prints, but he couldn't be sure of that.

Ingleby drew the weapon out by a piece of string which was tied round the shaft; a label was tied to it, too. He held it up in front of Mannering, dangling from the piece of string. "That was stuffed into the pocket of the injured man," the detective asserted. "The pocket of his trousers was smeared with blood, too. The handle has been wiped clear of prints, so no positive identification of the person who last used it can be made, but—" he let the rest of what he was going to say hover in the air.

Mannering said: "So he hit himself, and stuffed that into his pocket."

Ingleby jumped up. "No, Mr. Mannering, he didn't hit himself, and if you think this is the proper moment for facetiousness, I don't. One man brutally murdered, another as brutally attacked, the second man found in your apartment with the weapon cleaned of prints and stuffed into the victim's pocket—is *that* funny? Go on, tell me, is that funny?" Ingleby's eyes were glittering, he was swinging the hammer almost as if he would like to use it. "Now, let's have the truth, Mannering—what have you been doing with the men involved in these crimes? Why is it happening?" He strode forward and thrust a pointing finger in front of Mannering's nose. "Go on, tell me that? What have you been playing with fire for? Where are the Laker jewels? Come along, tell me—where are the jewels which Rett Laker stole, fifteen years ago, which he hid away, and sold to you after he came out of prison?"

Mannering said: "Take your hand away from my face." He waited for a split second, then pushed Ingleby's hand aside. "Raise your voice at me again and I'll put you outside. Don't think that being a policeman will help you."

Ingleby glowered. "So now you're threatening *me*."

"I'm telling you to behave like a civilised human being."

"There's nothing civilised about smashing a man's skull."

"There's nothing civilised about ranting like a pocket dictator, either."

Ingleby drew further back, and his expression was livid.

"My God," he said. "If I ever get you for this, I'll make you suffer."

"You'd be a better policeman if you just worried about getting the murderer. No man in his senses would carry out a murderous attack when he was expecting the police."

"He might, if the man he attacked could do him harm with the authorities."

"If he feared that, he would make sure he was dead."

"Or rely on convincing the police that he was innocent."

"If you really think like this, you oughtn't to be on the Force," Mannering said sharply.

Ingleby swung round. "All right," he growled. "You've asked for it." He reached the half-open door, and Mannering remembered that the landing door was also ajar. "Dickinson!" called Ingleby, his voice still thick with anger. "Come in and get started." Ingleby stood with his back to Mannering, who was almost certain what the unknown Dickinson was to start. "Bring the others in, and get a move on."

Mannering jumped to his feet, strode across the room, saw Ingleby start to turn round, hearing him; pushed the C.I.D. man vigorously to one side, and ran across the hall. He reached the door as it began to open wider. A thickset plainclothes man was standing just outside, looking down the stairs to two others who came hurrying up. Mannering said savagely: "Mind your hand," and slammed the door; Dickinson snatched his hand away from the doorway just in time. Mannering fastened the catch of the door, and turned round to see Ingleby staring towards him, eyes glittering with rage.

"Have you gone crazy? Impeding the police in the course of—"

"Have you a search warrant?"

"I don't need a search warrant after finding that man here."

"You've got the man, you've got the weapon. From now on you need a search warrant."

Ingleby was momentarily shaken.

"I can damned soon get one."

"Then go and get one, and when you've got it signed by a magistrate you can come here and search," Mannering said, harshly. "Provided you behave like a human being instead of like an idiot."

"Mannering, you'll regret this."

"Ingleby," Mannering said, in a low-pitched but very clear voice, "the only thing I have to regret is that I once gave you a helping hand. Try to get some simple facts into your head. I have never heard of Rett Laker's jewels. I had never heard of Laker until this afternoon. I had never met his niece until this afternoon either, and then I saw her at her own request. I had never met Samuel Blest until after his death. While you're getting your search warrant you might try reciting those facts until you've learned them off by heart."

He unlatched the door, opened it wide, and stood aside for Ingleby to go out. Dickinson and two other plain-clothes men, who must have heard every word, were standing on the landing, obviously not sure what to do, and waiting for instructions. Mannering was still seething, but at the same time telling himself that it would not help if he lost his temper, or if he stood too much on his dignity. But he had taken this stand, and couldn't shift his ground.

He heard the whining sound of the lift, and wondered who was coming up. It stopped at a floor below, and the silence seemed intense. Ingleby was breathing hard through his nostrils, as if he could not make up his mind what attitude to adopt. Every moment he lost was a moment's gain for Mannering, although if Ingleby went for a search warrant, when he came back he would be ruthlessly thorough.

Then Mannering heard footsteps on the stairs.

Ingleby said: "Wait outside here, sergeant. I'll be back with that warrant in less than half an hour. Make sure that no one comes in or goes out of the flat, by the back or the front."

From the foot of the flight of stairs, Lorna Mannering called:

"Does that include me, Mr. Ingleby?"

Lorna turned the bend in the stairs, and came towards them. She was tall and slim, with a good figure, and just now she was beautifully dressed in a suit which had come from Patelli; a ridiculously attractive little hat seemed to throw up her dark hair to glossy perfection. She moved as lightly and easily as she spoke, and she was smiling as if knowing that only she could hope to break this tension.

"Because I belong here," she said, and reached the landing. She looked at Mannering. "Hallo, darling, I didn't know that you had guests."

7

LORNA

LORNA did Mannering so much good that he could have laughed aloud. Instead, he put his hands to her and drew her into the flat, while Dickinson tried to look the other way, and Ingleby seemed bereft of words for the first time this night.

"Not exactly guests," Mannering said. "They seem to think that I clouted a man over the head with a plumber's hammer."

"And didn't you?" inquired Lorna.

"Not this time."

"I never did believe in treating burglars too leniently," Lorna said. "You mustn't get sentimental about thieves or policemen, sweet. Must he, Mr. Ingleby? Are you coming or going?"

"He's going," said Mannering, "but he's coming back shortly. With a search warrant."

"How tiresome," Lorna said. "I must get to bed quickly, then I'll have an oasis of peace and quiet."

Her bland good humour was too much for Ingleby and his men. Ingleby said something under his breath, and turned away and started down the stairs. The others followed. When they were half-way down Ingleby spoke in a muffled voice, but his words were clear enough; he was telling two of them to stay near the Mannering's flat, one on the first landing, one in the hall. All three of them disappeared.

Mannering drew Lorna further in, and closed the door. She was smiling at him, head on one side. But Mannering knew what Ingleby would not have guessed in a hundred years; she was very anxious, and that showed in her eyes.

Mannering said: "Come and have a drink, darling,"

and led the way to the study, which was their living-room when they were on their own. "Or do you want to take your hat off first?"

"I think I'll slip into a dressing-gown," Lorna said. "Mary fed me far too well, and something at dinner was blowy-outy. Come and tell me all about it while I change."

She led the way into their bedroom, where Ethel had already drawn the blinds, and switched on a subdued light. Mannering sat back in her sewing chair, and watched as she unfastened the zip at the back of her blouse, shrugged it over her shoulders, and then stepped out of her skirt. She was beautifully proportioned—not a small woman, not really slim, but certainly not heavy. She loosened the brassière at her full, white breasts, and it dangled down tantalisingly as she went across to a cupboard for her dressing-gown. Her movements were quick and light. She put the dressing-gown on, turned her back on him, unzipped and then wriggled clear of her girdle. Then she pulled on a pair of pyjama trousers, and tied the dressing-gown; then buttoned it high at the neck.

"So that's how it happened," she said, drily.

"I haven't said a word," protested Mannering, and laughed. "All right, all right, I know that's what you meant. I am what is called preoccupied."

"You mean you're worried."

After a pause, Mannering responded quietly: "Yes, darling, I think I am. Partly because I don't know what it's all about. Care for that drink?"

"Just hand me some indigestion tablets," Lorna pleaded.

As he went across to her dressing-table, to get a bottle, she went on: "Did I play the fool too much?"

Mannering laughed.

"If you hadn't, I think I would have crowned Ingleby. I'd already thrown him out of the flat. You couldn't have timed it better or eased the tension more." He watched her sitting back on her bed, hitching the pillows behind her, and put his legs up on a stool. This was a late night and early morning habit of intimacy between them, although more often than not she was drinking tea when they sat like this. "It's one of the oddest affairs," Mannering began, and told her exactly what had happened.

He did not know that he impressed her most by the complete control that he had of the facts, the way he marshalled the details into their proper order; nothing could have made it more convincing that he was not only worried by the situation but had given it a great deal of intense thought. At least the tension was gone, and he was not continually looking over his shoulder towards the door; nor was he alert for the sound of the front door bell. Yet half an hour must have passed between Ingleby's departure, and the time of the finishing of the recital.

Lorna said slowly: "And the man got upstairs, darling."

"He might have used the lift," Mannering said. "He almost certainly did. Why didn't you, by the way?"

"I saw a policeman downstairs and thought I heard voices up here, so it seemed better to listen and walk," answered Lorna. "Do you think the man who came here was the one who telephoned you?"

"It's possible."

"Wasn't his voice the same?"

"He didn't really use his voice when he came here, he only muttered incoherently," Mannering said. "The worst of the situation is that he couldn't walk. He would never have got across the flat if I hadn't helped him. He was leaning against the wall, almost as if someone had propped him there." He caught his breath, and his eyes narrowed. "As if someone had propped him there," he repeated, very softly. "That could be it. If someone wanted him to be found in the flat, badly injured and looking as if he'd been attacked here, that's what they would do."

"Darling," Lorna said, and burped slightly. "Sorry."

"Yes?"

"Why should anyone want to do that?"

"I can't even begin to guess."

"How serious *is* it?"

Mannering said grimly: "Serious enough for Ingleby to get a warrant for my arrest if that's the way the police want it. Look at the situation cold-bloodedly, sweet." As he spoke, the full significance of the words struck at him. He felt his heart beginning to pound again, and saw the deepening anxiety in Lorna's eyes. Cold-bloodedly was the only way he could look at the situation, and seen like that, it scared him. "This man couldn't walk. The two doctors didn't say much, but they both said: 'I can't imagine how he managed to get here.' That must have started Ingleby's mind ticking over, and for some reason he already thought that I was interested in a cache of jewels which the man Laker had stashed away. A man so badly wounded that he could not have walked up those stairs and probably could not have operated the automatic lift, was found in this flat, with the weapon in his pocket, wiped clear of prints. Imagine what I would think if I heard this about someone else."

Lorna said: "I don't want to."

"I know what we both want," Mannering said. "And what I need most is two or three days in which to move around and find out what's going on, but it wouldn't surprise me if the police make sure that I can't."

"Have they really enough to make a charge?"

"Yes, I think they could justify one. A defence counsel might be able to make hay of it, but—well, grant that the injured man could implicate me in a serious crime, and had to be silenced, and there's a case."

"But he isn't dead!"

"The police could argue that I thought he was." When Lorna made no comment, Mannering went on: "The only bright spot is the fact that Ingleby was ready to wait for a search warrant. If they found any of these jewels on the premises I'd spend the night in a police station cell." He moistened his lips, and looked round at the door, then back at Lorna; and he knew that the same question was forming in her mind.

She uttered it.

"They can't find any of the jewels here, can they?"

"If you'd asked me an hour ago, I would have said that they couldn't find a man with a smashed skull here, or that you couldn't find the hammer used to hit him with. I'd be flabbergasted if any jewels were found, but—"

He broke off, and caught his breath. Lorna asked quickly:

"What is it, John?" When he didn't answer, she leaned forward and demanded again: "What have you thought of?"

Mannering said: "If that hammer was in the injured man's pocket, some jewels could have been, too. I don't know what he was coming to see me about. If it was the man who telephoned for an appointment in Hyde Park, he might have had the real Blest jewellery."

"But surely—" Lorna broke off, equally aghast.

"Yes?"

"But surely if Ingleby had found anything like that in the man's pockets, he would have told you by now—or else he would have taken you with him."

"Not necessarily," Mannering said. "He might judge it wiser to take them to the Yard for identification. Jewels as jewels wouldn't be significant. They would matter only if they were stolen." He stood up from the sewing chair, went to Lorna's long mirror, looked at his reflection in it, and saw Lorna's reflection, too. She was quite beautiful, but pale and very anxious—nearly as anxious as he. He felt as if a net was tightening round him, and that there was nothing at all he could do to free himself—he could not even see where the next strand of the net would tighten. "I'd give a lot to know what they're thinking at the Yard," he went on. "There isn't much doubt that they could put me on a charge."

.   .   .   .

Chief Inspector Ingleby had worked at New Scotland Yard long enough to feel no awkwardness whenever he went there from the Division. Most of the senior and many of the junior officers were old friends of his, and usually he enjoyed an excuse for a visit. He was not greatly enjoying himself tonight. His suspicions of Mannering were very strong and fully justified, and yet there were imponderable factors which made him uneasy and uncertain of himself. Mannering's reputation, for instance, was so good that it was almost inconceivable that he would allow himself to become involved in dealing in stolen jewels, and with murder—but certain pieces of evidence were irrefutable. After leaving Mannering's flat, Ingleby had radioed the Yard and asked if it would be possible to see Chief Superintendent William Bristow. Bristow was the doyen of Yard superintendents, he was the specialist in precious stones, and he knew Mannering very well. Some said that the two men were close friends.

What Ingleby did not know—and what very few at the Yard even suspected—was that in their early days Bristow and Mannering had been on opposite sides of the fence. Bristow was the one person in England who was quite sure that Mannering had once been a jewel thief known as the Baron. There had never been proof; but all his life Bristow had believed that one day events might establish that proof, probably when it was least expected.

Ingleby went into a small office which had been made available for him for the evening, and immediately asked a detective sergeant on duty:

"Is Mr. Bristow coming?"

"He's on his way."

"Good," said Ingleby. "That means I'd better look slippy." He sat down at a bare-topped table, and made notes in a good, flowing hand, putting them in chronological order much as Mannering had done for Lorna. Finished, Ingleby telephoned the Westminster Hospital, where the injured man had been taken. A policeman on duty there to answer inquiries reported:

"They're operating, Mr. Ingleby, but no news has come through yet."

"Telephone me at the Yard if there's any word," Ingleby said. "Extension 524—and if I'm not there, ask for Mr. Bristow."

"Right, sir."

Ingleby rang off.

He had recovered from his exasperation and annoyance, and wondered whether Mannering realised that he had deliberately heightened the tension between them, acting as if he was much more angry than he had in fact been; his sole purpose had been to try to make Mannering lose his temper. He hadn't succeeded altogether. Now Ingleby lit a cigarette, thought longingly of the drink Mannering had offered, and browsed a little nostalgically about being stationed at the Yard. It was the hub of the Metropolitan C.I.D. and a Divisional job would never be quite the same.

The door opened, and Bristow came in.

He was a man of medium height, not particularly massive, with regular features which somehow failed to make him good-looking. He had a close-clipped grey moustache, the middle of which was stained yellow with nicotine, and in his well-cut grey jacket he wore a fresh-looking gardenia. Bristow's nicotined moustache and his gardenia were bywords at the Yard, and no one here now took the slightest notice of them. He had a quick, brisk manner and brisk movements; he shook hands briefly with Ingleby, pulled up an armchair, and invited:

"Tell me all about it."

Ingleby reported, making frequent references to his notes. It was quite impossible to judge Bristow's reaction. The Yard man smoked a cigarette and a half during the recital, and the only movement he made was to take a cigarette from his mouth and tap the ash off into the fireplace.

". . . and that's about it," Ingleby said, at last. "I had Mannering worried, I'm quite sure about that." When Bristow made no comment, he went on almost uneasily:

"The question is, sir, is there enough for a charge against Mannering?"

"Good God, yes!"

"That's what I thought," said Ingleby.

"Wouldn't put it past Mannering to have hit that man if he'd come to raid the flat," Bristow went on, and lit a third cigarette from the stub of his second. "But his story sounds reasonable—and it's hardly the kind of yarn he would spin if he were trying to cover up some crime."

"You mean, you believe it?"

"Too early to say what I believe yet," said Bristow. "You say that you think Mannering was badly shaken when you pointed out the fact that this injured man might have been attacked in his flat."

"He was shaken all right."

"Wouldn't be likely to be so shaken if he really had done the thing," Bristow pointed out, reasonably. "But that isn't much to do with whether we ought to charge him or not. Apart from the hammer, did you find anything else on the injured man?"

Ingleby pointed to some oddments placed out on a small table: keys, money, wallet, ticket, some letters, two handkerchiefs, a book of matches, a shoe-lace, and a piece of white chalk.

"That's the lot, sir. His name's Joe Farmer."

"Any record?"

"No, nothing known against him. I checked just before you arrived. And he's still alive."

"If he dies, Mannering could find himself on a murder charge," Bristow said. "The only charge we could prefer if we pulled him in now would be causing grievous bodily harm. I'd have been happier if we could have found some jewels at Mannering's place. If this chap could have proved him a fence, then Mannering might have taken the risk and attacked him. It would be more convincing if the man was dead, but he may have looked pretty dead, and if it happened that way Mannering would have been racing against time. He's pretty cagey, you know;

there isn't any way he can get stuff out of his flat, is there?"

"I think I've made sure of that," answered Ingleby.

"Good. The first thing is to get that search warrant, and while we're at it, we'll get one for Quinns," Bristow decided. "If we find anything, we'll hold Mannering for the night at least. What else have you done?"

"Else?" Ingleby looked startled. "Well—"

"This girl, Rebecca Blest."

"She's being looked after by the neighbours downstairs, some people named Ashton. There's a daughter of about Rebecca Blest's age to keep her company." Ingleby seemed pleased with this report. "Young Terence McKay has gone home. To make sure there's no collusion between them and Mannering, I've started to check if they knew one another before. As far as I can find out, the girl did go to Mannering with these jewels of Laker's, only to find that they were false, and Terence McKay did meet the girl for the first time this afternoon—I haven't discovered any evidence that they knew each other before. That part of everybody's story seems to be true."

"Any motive established for the murder of Samuel Blest?"

"Nothing at all."

"Right," said Bristow, crisply. "You go and fix that search warrant, and say I'm ready to support it. I'll lay on a couple of good men to go along with you—men who know Mannering's flat," Bristow added drily. "And when the flat's been searched, you can go over to Quinns."

"Mr. Bristow," Ingleby said, and then hesitated.

"Yes?"

"You're not at all sure about Mannering being in the clear, are you?"

"It wouldn't be the first time that Mannering had got himself into a jam by trying to be quixotic," Bristow said gruffly, "and it wouldn't be the first time that Mannering handled stolen jewels in a kind of juggling act. I wouldn't put it past him to be trying to get the real jewels back in place of the false ones for this Rebecca Blest girl. Unusual name, isn't it? What's she like?"

"She's a sweetie," Ingleby said. "About twenty-three, and just the kind of girl I'd like my son to marry."

"Couldn't give me a better description," Bristow said. "You couldn't describe a better bait for Mannering, either. I wonder if these crooks are making a fool out of him." Under his breath he added what he so often thought: "One of these days his past will catch up with him."

8

PART OF THE PAST

Josh Larraby, the manager of Quinns, was part of Mannering's past, in much the same way as Bristow, although they were at extreme ends of the scale. Larraby had one love, which seemed to have been born in him, and which had strengthened over the years: a love for precious stones. He had worked for years with a West End jeweller, and the passion had developed into a craving and the craving into a mania, until the time had come when he had stolen a number of superbly beautiful jewels—and been caught.

That should have been his ruin.

After he had served his years of imprisonment, he had gone to Mannering for help. Against the advice of the police and his friends, Mannering had given the ex-convict a job at Quinns. That was over twelve years ago, and during those twelve years Larraby had been promoted from odd-job man to messenger, from messenger to general assistant, and finally to manager of the shop. It no longer occurred to Mannering that there might be the slightest reason for distrusting Larraby, and he believed that the police also felt sure that Larraby was completely honest.

Larraby was now in the middle sixties, rather frail-looking, with curly hair which had turned almost white, and a rather deceptively pale face and gentle expression; a kind of universal uncle of a man.

That night, he had left Covent Garden a little after ten o'clock, humming a tune to himself, having been pleasantly entertained by a reasonably good performance of *Figaro*. He would have walked home had it been earlier; as it was, he went to the Strand, took a Number 15 bus, got off opposite Selfridges and walked through Mayfair towards the mews where he had his small flat.

London was part of life to Larraby. Its pavements, its medley of buildings, its noises, its silences, its lights and its shadows, its smells and its vastness, all seemed natural to him, and he did not know what it was to feel nervous. He turned into the mews, walking over the cobbles without making much noise with his rubber-soled shoes, and taking out his keys as he reached the front door. On his ring were keys not only of the flat, but of Quinns' front door. Only he and Mannering could get into Quinns; no one else had keys.

Larraby pushed the front door open, and went in, closing the door behind him, for there was a lamp in the mews opposite the door, and the light shone through the frosted glass panel. He was still humming when he kicked against something stretched across the passage. He pitched headlong, taken absolutely by surprise, alarmed in that moment only by the fall. Crashing down, he turned to one side so that he took the worst of the blow on his right shoulder, but could not prevent his head from banging on the floor. That caused a wave of pain which nearly made him unconscious. He lay helpless for what seemed a long time. Suddenly, without a second's warning, a light went on.

Through the tears of pain in his eyes Larraby could see a man's feet; suddenly one moved, and he felt the pointed toe bury itself in his shoulder. He cried aloud with greater pain, now much more badly frightened.

"Get up," a man ordered, roughly.

The pain seemed to be spreading from Larraby's head throughout his whole body, and he had no strength in his arms or in his legs. He tried to scramble to his feet, but could not. He felt a hand at the collar of his coat, pinching painfully, and was hauled to his feet and pushed roughly to one side. He thumped against a wall, and would have fallen but for its support. The pain in his head was still excruciating, especially at the back of his eyes, and he could see only with difficulty. But he was able to make out the shape of two men, one of them in the doorway of his bed-sitting room, the other near the front door.

The man by the door said: "Take his keys."

Larraby tried to back away, but he could not; the man nearer him pulled him forward by the shoulder, spun him round, and thrust a hand into his trousers pockets. He found the keys at the second attempt, and drew them out, jingling. Then he waved them in front of Larraby's eyes, so that the brightness sent scintillas of light stabbing from them, as if they were jewels.

"Now listen, Larraby," said the man by the door. "We're going for a little ride. We're going to Quinns. We're going to break in, and you're going to open the strong-room for us. If you try any tricks or make any trouble, you'll have your skull cracked in like Humpty Dumpty." He drew his hand from his pocket, and held up a hammer; Larraby did not know that it was exactly like the hammer which Ingleby had found earlier in the evening, but he did remember that vicious kick, and the pain now easing in his head.

"Got all that?" the man demanded roughly.

Larraby muttered: "Yes. Yes, I've got it."

His head was hurting too much for him to think clearly, but one thing was certain: he could not do anything to help himself here. It would take some time to go to the shop, and to get inside—and by that time he would probably be feeling better, and be much more able to cope. There were devices at the shop which could be called on to raise an alarm—devices which he and Mannering had developed to meet such an eventuality as this. At the moment he must do what he was told. Especially, he must avoid further violence. He had to use every second in order to recover his strength and his nerve.

"Make sure you don't try any tricks," the man said. "Or else—"

He raised the hammer suddenly and violently. Larraby backed away—and with a backward sweep, the man smashed the head of the hammer down on a picture on the wall. The glass shattered. Tiny slivers like darts stuck in the wall, into the man's clothes, even into his hair. The man himself was startled, and swung round. His expression showed the viciousness and the brutality in him. He recovered quickly, and said: "We'll get that cleared up—send Blackie to do it. Now, Larraby, if you don't want your head cracked like that glass—" He broke off.

Larraby moistened his lips.

"I'll do whatever you tell me."

"The first thing is you'll walk out of here with my pal, and go to the car across the mews," ordered the man with the hammer. "Just get in the back, like he tells you. Pretend he's a friend of yours."

Larraby didn't speak as he began to obey.

The man with the hammer opened the door, and the light from across the way showed clearly on the white-washed walls of the other houses in the mews. Light glowed yellow and friendly at two square windows, and a car passed the end of the mews, heading for Oxford Street. Larraby saw a Vauxhall car parked where the man had said. The other man took his arm, above the elbow, gripping him painfully, and started across the cobbles. Larraby made no attempt to get free. He sat in a corner of the car, edging over as the other man got in beside him. Then the one with the hammer came out of the flat, slammed the door, and walked boldly across and took the wheel. Larraby saw his big hands with their tough-looking, spatulate fingers and nails bitten down almost to the quick. The man started the car and drove off with a kind of restrained strength which told of the brute in him. He swung round the corner out of the mews too quickly, and a cyclist swerved to avoid him. "Bloody bikes," he swore, and then put his foot hard down on the accelerator.

Larraby thought: *The police will stop him.*

The man seemed to wake up to the risk he was taking, and slowed down. It was only a five-minute drive to Quinns, but he drove past the end of Hart Row and glanced along it, as if to make sure that no one was lurking there, then took the next turning to the right. So he knew there was another way to the car park. He stopped the car at the far end of Hart Row, and switched off the lights and the engine. Now only the single lamp near Quinns spread light, but there was diffused glow from Bond Street. Little traffic passed.

The man with the hammer said: "Okay, Fred."

The man named Fred opened his door, said: "Out," and then pulled Larraby with him. Larraby got out. The night air struck cold at his bare head and his face, and he shivered. He could see the narrow front of Quinns, could even make out the name in gilt lettering on the dark fascia board above the shop. The other man got out, and they ranged on either side of Larraby, powerful and menacing.

The leader said: "Go and open the door. Don't go in— just open the door. Don't forget, we'll be watching." After a pause, he added: "Go with him, Fred."

"Okay."

"You know what to do if he tries to pull a fast one."

"I know what to do."

"And I'll finish him off," the leader said.

Larraby felt himself shivering uncontrollably as he went to the front door. He could get into the shop, and there was just a chance that he could push the door open, dash in, and close the door on the man. But if he tried that and failed, would they have any mercy on him?

He did not think they would.

He reached the porch, remembering how he had closed and locked the door this very evening, after Mannering had left. *Mannering.* He owed more to the proprietor of Quinns than to anyone living, and would make any sacrifice for him. Yet his fear was agonising. Only a few years ago, his predecessor in management had been murdered in a raid on the shop, and when Larraby had taken over the job, Mannering had talked to him, in that office at the back.

It was almost possible to hear his words.

"Josh, I don't care what the circumstances are, I don't want you or anyone else killed trying to protect anything at Quinns. Is that clear? If it ever becomes a question of letting thieves get away with a haul, or risking your life, let them get away with it. You know as well as I do that nine times out of ten they won't stay free for long, and we'll get the stolen things back. If we don't, we're fully insured. So never take risks with your life, Josh. That's a condition of the job. Understand?"

Larraby had said: "I fully understand, Mr. Mannering."

Never take risks with your life, Josh.

Supposing he made the attempt to lock these men out, and failed? They would certainly make him suffer for it, and might kill. But would they let him live, even if he did what they wanted? He could identify them. He would be a damning witness against them, and because of that they would probably kill him before they left. He could take that almost for granted; they would use him to get inside the shop and the strong-room, and afterwards they would kill him. So he would not be taking risks with his life; the risk was already there. If he tried to shut these men out, however, he would be fighting for a chance to live.

Never take risks with your life, Josh.

Larraby felt the man named Fred breathing down his neck as he used the keys on the double lock, and pressed the secret mechanism which would allow him to open the door without an alarm going off. His one chance would be to thrust the door wide open without making any sound, then to hack at the man's shins. He needed only a split second.

He felt the door yielding, under the pressure of his trembling hand.

9

LARRABY TRIES

LARRABY knew that he had to make an attempt to save Quinns.

He felt the door yield, and steeled himself to thrust it wide open, and to kick backwards at the man just behind him. He had actually started to push when he felt a vicious kick at the back of his right leg. His knee gave way, and he almost fell. The man grabbed him by the arm, held him up, and pushed him inside the shop. He went staggering, fetched up against the corner of a Genoese silver table, and gasped as a corner cut into him. He managed to save himself from falling, and in the few seconds which followed saw the other two men come in, and heard the door close. They caught up with him. For a moment he thought that they would attack him then and there; but each man took an arm, and they hoisted him off the ground and carried him between them to the end of the shop. A light glowed there, to show patrolling police that all was well. Beyond this was the doorway to Mannering's study; a small recess led to it. The two men pushed Larraby into the recess, and pressed against him, so that they could not be seen from the street.

The man with the hammer said: "Unlock Mannering's office."

"I—I can't do it," Larraby muttered. "I can't—"

The man said: "You'll open that office and then you'll open the strong-room, and if you try any tricks you won't live to see another day."

Larraby's hands were even more unsteady, and he kept shivering. Mannering's instructions became very vivid in his mind, however, and for the first time tonight he began to wonder if these men would let him go; he

70

began to hope that he might live. He knew exactly what keys to use for the door; he knew exactly how to open the strong-room door. Only he and Mannering had the secret of the electronics and the electrical control; as he began to insert his key in the door, he wished vainly that Mannering had never instructed him in their use.

The office door opened.

"Inside," ordered the man with the hammer, and pushed Larraby in. The big, brutish man stepped in after him, quickly, and closed the door. The man named Fred was left outside, keeping watch; if there were any threat from the street, he would raise the alarm.

Larraby watched the thickset man with the hammer, which he kept weighing up and down in his hand.

"Now get busy, Larraby," he said. "Just get busy."

Everything in Larraby screamed out against what he was about to do, but all the time there was that insistent command of Mannering's. *Never take risks with your life, Josh.* The place was fully insured, and in any case there was not a great deal of easily negotiable jewellery and small works of art in the strong-room. To have even a faint chance to live, Larraby knew, he had to open that door.

"Now!" the man rasped.

Larraby's lips were working. He hated himself for what he was about to do, but—they *might* let him live. He did not really think they would, but if he disobeyed the man with the hammer he would throw what little chance there was away.

He kept muttering to himself, as if he were praying.

.   .   .   .

Mannering was still sitting in the bedroom, with Lorna, when the front door bell rang. Neither of them moved for a moment; they stared at each other in attempted mutual reassurance. Then Mannering got up, moved to the side of the bed, bent over his wife, and put his lips close to hers. "Sorry, my darling," he said, and kissed her. He felt the pressure of her lips against his. Then he turned away abruptly, as the front door bell rang again. He felt sure that it was Ingleby, and he was right. Ingleby had two other men with him; Mannering recognised them both as from the Yard, men who usually worked with Bristow. He wondered glumly if Bristow had been consulted, and whether he was outside, as he let Ingleby in.

Ingleby took the search warrant from his pocket.

"All right, you carry on," Mannering said. "Make as little mess as you can, won't you?"

"I have no desire to exceed my duty," Ingleby declared, in spite of his anxiety, Mannering could have laughed. "Has Mrs. Mannering retired?"

"Yes."

"If she will be good enough to leave her room for a quarter of an hour we will get that done as quickly as we can," Ingleby said formally.

Mannering went to tell Lorna.

They sat together in the study while the police moved about the apartment, the unfamiliar heavy footsteps sounding very loud.

Ethel, who had come in just before Ingleby, accepted the situation with a kind of scared good grace, and Mannering heard Ingleby questioning her. He wouldn't get much change out of Ethel, who had worked for the Mannerings long enough to know that involvement in the investigation of crime was normal.

After twenty minutes, Lorna was told that she could return to her bedroom. Mannering closed the door on her and went to the drawing-room, a long, narrow chamber of green and gold, which had already been searched. Two pictures were askew, an indication that every picture had been moved, while the cushions on the chairs and couches weren't exactly as Lorna would have liked them. No damage had been done, however. Ingleby was making sure that there was no cause for complaint.

Mannering felt more edgy with every passing minute, although he felt reasonably sure that nothing but the hammer had been found on the injured man. As the work went on, and there were no sensations, he began to feel convinced that nothing would be discovered at the flat—so, nothing had been hidden here.

If the police were prepared to take action on the strength of what they had discovered so far, surely they would have charged him, and carried out this search when he was in a police cell.

The trouble was that he could not be sure, and his mood of disquiet increased. He would be less troubled if he could discern some pattern in all that had happened, see some reason for anyone to suggest that he was handling the Rett Laker jewels.

It was half-past eleven when Ingleby came to the door of the room.

"We've finished, Mr. Mannering."

"And drawn a complete blank, I trust."

"Didn't you expect us to?"

"I didn't expect you to find a hammer in the injured man's pocket. Do you know how he is?"

"The last I heard he was undergoing a brain operation," Ingleby answered. "There isn't likely to be any report of the result until tomorrow morning. I have another search warrant, Mr. Mannering." Ingleby seemed to use that as a threat.

Mannering said heavily: "The shop?"

"Yes."

"And you want me there," said Mannering. He thought of Josh Larraby, wondered fleetingly whether he should try to persuade the police to use Josh as their guide, and then changed his mind. It would be wiser to go himself.

.   .   .   .

Mannering sat beside Ingleby in a police car, with a plainclothes driver who took no chances but lost no time.

Except for a few couples, and one or two people on their own and walking briskly, no one was about, and New Bond Street's windows were either in darkness or garishly bright. As they swung round the corner into Hart Row, Ingleby exclaimed without warning:

"Slow down!"

The driver's foot was on the brake in an instant. Mannering turned his gaze away from Quinns, to see Ingleby twisting round in his seat and looking towards the side of the road.

"Turn round and let's get a good look at that chap over there," Ingleby ordered. "It looks like Tommy Glee. If he's out tonight, it isn't for fun."

"Who's Tommy Glee?" inquired Mannering, as the driver reversed with practised speed, and drove up New Bond Street again.

"A fur thief," Ingleby answered tersely.

They passed a solitary little man on the right hand side of the road; he was hurrying, and they could hear the sharp tap-tap of steel heel protectors. He turned his head towards a shop-window, and the driver said:

"That's Tommy all right."

"Flash the Yard," said Ingleby. "They'll keep tabs on him."

Mannering felt helpless as he sat listening to the squeaks and squawks, the buzzing and the voices on the radio. The message was received, and flashed to another car by the time this car reached Oxford Street's brighter lights. In all, they had lost no more than four minutes, but that was enough to give Mannering a vivid sense of the bustle of activity at the Yard, a glimpse of the long arm of the law stretching out in a dozen directions at once.

Quinns looked normal when they arrived.

Mannering opened the street door, and switched on some of the side lights which threw show cases into relief; jewels showed, fiery and bright, behind plate glass. The rest of the shop seemed shadowy and dark. Mannering led the way, with Ingleby just behind and keeping pace for pace, as if to make sure that Mannering could not steal a march. They reached the office, and Mannering stood in the doorway, before unlocking it. He was frowning.

"What's the matter?" demanded Ingleby.

"Can you smell tobacco smoke?"

"Faintly."

"No one should have been in here since half-past six," Mannering declared.

"Smoke hangs about for a long time," Ingleby pointed out.

Mannering said: "It doesn't stay as fresh as this for long." He switched on another light, which shone on to the office doorway, bent down, and inspected the brass escutcheon plate closely.

"Well?" demanded Ingleby.

"It's not been touched," Mannering said.

Ingleby gave a kind of snort, an indication of impatience. The other policemen were by the door, and Mannering was acutely conscious of the way they watched him. In spite of his efforts to keep absolutely steady, or perhaps because of them, he scraped the key on the plate. When he turned it, he did so too sharply, and the door did not open first time. He was behaving as if he had something on his conscience, whereas in fact only the mysteries of the night were heavy on his mind—and this latest pressed most heavily. He was virtually certain that someone had smoked in here within the last half-hour or so.

What would he find?

He opened the door at last, hesitated, put a hand to the light switch, and pressed it down; the light came on quite normally. He looked across at the corner, where shelves filled with heavy books concealed the entrance to the strong-room. As the policemen came in after him, big men who seemed to tread very heavily, he could smell tobacco smoke more pungent than ever.

Then he saw that two of the books which controlled the *ACTIVE* switch of the electronic control were a few inches out of place on the middle shelf, standing out from the other books. Now he was certain that something was badly wrong.

Only Larraby knew about those particular books.

"Someone's been in here since the shop was closed tonight," Mannering insisted.

"I've known smoke to hang about for days," declared Ingleby.

"I don't mean only the smoke," Mannering said, and explained about the books. Ingleby was obviously sceptical, and the other two stared at him unbelievingly— unless his imagination was playing him tricks?

"Are you saying that you can't open the strong-room door?" demanded Ingleby.

"I can open it," Mannering said. "I think the place has been broken into already."

"You'll soon know," Ingleby said tartly, and the driver coughed.

Mannering pulled the books right out, his mind working very fast, but also in agitation. He did not believe that anyone could have stumbled upon the secret by chance; and Larraby would never have talked about it. There seemed only one answer to the urgent questions. Larraby had been forced to open the strong-room—and so as to warn Mannering at the earliest possible moment, had left those particular books out of position.

It was no use trying to persuade Ingleby of that.

That wasn't the only anxiety, for—where was Larraby?

Mannering switched off the electronic control, and the electric locking and alarm devices, then used two keys in the double lock in the wall behind the two books. He stood back.

"Well?" Ingleby demanded harshly.

"I press the last control switch, and the wall pivots open," Mannering explained, and pressed. A section of the book-shelves moved, the top going backwards, the bottom forward. Through the gap at the bottom they could see a flight of stairs leading downwards.

"This is as near burglar-proof as anything I know," said Ingleby, grudgingly. "I'll go first, please."

Mannering let him, and followed after, putting on the light, fearful of seeing Larraby injured or dead, or some sign of a raid. There was none. The individual safes were all closed, and presumably locked. Small works of art and some less valuable pieces stood on shelves, pictures hung from the ceiling along two sides, and the big day safe, in which goods were put for temporary custody, did not appear to have been tampered with.

Then those two books—

"Open the big one first, will you?" asked Ingleby.

Mannering obeyed, pulled open the heavy door, and stood to one side. Among the first of the pieces which Ingleby took out were some of those which Rebecca Blest had brought—the simple move which had begun all this.

One of them, the bracelet, flashed with light so brilliant that it made Ingleby move nearer to a lamp, and one of the men exclaim.

Mannering stood thunderstruck.

That bracelet wasn't a fake. It was the real thing.

He stood stiff, and unbelieving, as Ingleby took out more of Rebecca Blest's collection. Piece after piece was passed from one policeman to another, and then tension developed into fierce excitement.

Mannering knew why.

All these jewels were real; even the settings were genuinely old. Ingleby and his men were fully aware of that, and also knew that these were some of the jewels stolen by Rett Laker.

The police had found exactly what they had hoped to find—all the evidence they needed that Quinns was being used to harbour stolen goods. No one would be convinced when Mannering told the truth—that fake jewellery had been taken away from here and the genuine put in its place.

10

ARREST

INGLEBY held a necklace close to his eyes, and seemed to linger over the stones lovingly, as if touched by a kindred passion to that which Larraby and Mannering felt for precious stones. He stood very still for a long time, then handed the jewels to one of the others, who took them almost reverently. The third policeman gave a nervous snort of a laugh.

At last, Ingleby spoke.

"Are these the fake jewels, Mr. Mannering?"

Mannering said: "No, they're not fakes." After the first moment of shock, he felt more able to cope; now that he knew the worst he was in much more control of himself, and his voice was steadier. "They're genuine—the jewels as well as the settings."

"And yet you—"

"I've never seen them before," Mannering asserted.

The policeman who had given the snort of a laugh did so again.

"You've never seen jewellery which was safely locked away in your own strong-room?" asked Ingleby; his voice dripped with disbelief. "Perhaps you could explain how they came to be here."

Only Josh Larraby could have opened the strong-room and left so little sign that anyone had raided it, Mannering reminded himself. *Josh. Loyal Josh.* Mannering remembered all that had happened between them in the past, in a single swift kaleidoscopic vision—Josh, straight from jail, deeply grateful for a chance to rehabilitate himself, winning a reputation for honesty, and at last fully trusted in the trade.

"Can you, Mr. Mannering?" insisted Ingleby.

Mannering said: "No, not yet."

"You never will," muttered the snorter.

"But I've never seen them before," Mannering repeated. Even to him this sounded ridiculous. "Miss Blest brought me roughly made glass replicas of all these, set in imitation settings. I put them in this strong-room myself." He remembered the grubby little bags and grubby cotton wool in which the stones had been wrapped, and now began to ask himself questions. The first and obvious one was: why should anyone put the real jewels in place of the old? Robbery in reverse did not make sense. But somewhere behind all this lurked sense: a cold, cunning, considered intelligence had directed this thing.

"Take that statement down, sergeant, will you?" ordered Ingleby. Immediately, one of the men made a great fuss of taking a notebook and pencil from his pocket. "Mr. Mannering states that these jewels are unfamiliar to him—is that it, Mr. Mannering?"

"Let's have it right," Mannering said. "I have never seen the jewels before, but I have seen imitations which were brought to me by Miss Rebecca Blest this afternoon."

"And—" invited Ingleby. He sounded as if he was on top of the world.

"I have no idea how these came to be in my strong-room."

"Can't you make a suggestion, Mr. Mannering?"

"No," Mannering replied. "I've nothing more to say."

"Well, I have," said Ingleby, and his voice roughened. "John Mannering, it is my duty to charge you with being in possession of precious stones knowing them to be stolen, and I must warn you that anything you say may be taken down and used in evidence."

There was utter silence, until the policeman gave that snort of a laugh again; but it wasn't really gloating, he was suffering from suppressed excitement. Ingleby was gloating, though; he looked as puffed up as a toy balloon.

"Have you anything to say?" His voice rang out.

"Not yet," Mannering said, with difficulty, "except to

deny that these jewels were here with my knowledge."

He chose each word most carefully, while all the time he seemed to see Josh Larraby's eyes, clear, trustful, trusting—and he saw those two books standing out a little from the shelf. The sinister truth of what had happened was dawning on him, and taking effect slowly. He was under arrest. He would be brought up before the magistrate in the morning and charged with being in possession of stolen jewels, and—he would be remanded. His main hope, for the time being, was to be remanded on bail. There had been plenty of times in the past when he had been on the point of arrest, but he had never felt so certain that he would not escape the police court hearing.

There was *Lorna*.

He felt sticky and hot.

"Open the other safes, Mr. Mannering, will you," asked Ingleby. "We might as well make a job of it, now we're here."

Mannering thought: *Lorna*, in an empty kind of way, and took out his keys again, opened the safes, and watched as the police went through the contents, one by one. He knew every piece of jewellery, every miniature, every little *objet d'art* which was here for safe keeping. There were dozens of pieces which would have been worth stealing, and yet nothing had been touched; he would have found out during the search if anything at all had been taken away. Someone had broken in here, or been allowed in by Larraby, had taken the false Laker jewels and replaced them by the genuine ones, and then gone off, leaving a fortune untouched.

It simply didn't make sense.

Mannering reminded himself that only someone with a cold, keen intelligence could have planned a thing like this. So he would be bound to find out the reason, soon. It had been done with deliberate purpose, and that purpose was hanging over him like a weight that might drop and crush him at any moment.

Lorna.

Ingleby said: "If you wish to telephone your wife before we go, that will be permissible, Mr. Mannering."

"Ah," said Mannering. "Yes. Thanks."

. . . .

Lorna was dozing in bed when the telephone bell rang, and she sat up with a start, glanced at the bedside clock, and saw that it was after twelve o'clock. Why had John been so long? She leaned slowly sideways and picked up the telephone, jumpy because she had been startled, annoyed with herself because she had so nearly dropped off to sleep.

"Mrs. Mannering," she announced.

"Hallo, my sweet," John said, and although he spoke clearly and almost heartily, Lorna sensed on the instant that something was badly wrong; there was an attempt at reassurance in his voice which did not ring true.

"John!"

"Something has misfired," John went on, too easily. "Someone left some stolen jewels at Quinns tonight, and the police want me to explain what it's all about. I'm going over to the Yard now, and I don't think I'll be home until morning. I'll call you as soon after eight o'clock as I can. Sleep well."

"John, don't ring off." Lorna was sitting upright, her heart thumping. She could picture him sitting in that little sewing chair, overlapping it on each side, with the tea tray on a stool between him and the bed. "Just how serious is it?"

"It could be unpleasant," Mannering answered carefully, "but there's no need to take that for granted. I'd like the night to think about it, and if necessary we'll get Toby Pleydell over in the morning."

"John, are you—are you under arrest?"

There was a long pause, and Lorna wanted to cry: "*Are you?*" but made herself keep quiet.

John said, very quietly: "Yes, darling, but I'm not very worried about it."

"*You're* not worried!" she began, and choked the words back. It was bad enough for him already. She must not do anything to make the situation worse, but a dozen questions reared up in her mind. She couldn't just ring off and let things hang fire like this. John must talk to Toby Pleydell, their solicitor, now. If John were under arrest he had every right to. Under *arrest*! She thought of the man who had been injured, who might have been attacked in this very apartment, according to the police; and she thought of the man who had been murdered that afternoon. This wasn't simply a misunderstanding over stolen jewels, this was murder—and John was already under suspicion.

"Good night, sweet," Mannering said.

"John! I must call Toby—"

"I don't think it will help, tonight," Mannering said. "The morning will be time enough. I expect to see Bill Bristow soon, and I think I can convince him that the charge is a mistake. Try to take it easy for tonight."

Lorna began: "But John—" then swallowed the words, drew in a deep breath, and said: "Yes, of course I will. If you're not worried there's no reason why I should be. If you haven't telephoned by half-past eight in the morning, where shall I come?"

"Just check with the Yard," Mannering said.

"All—all right, John. And you try to get some sleep."

"I'll sleep like a log," Mannering assured her with that false heartiness. "Mind you do, too. Good night!"

He rang off, with that last absurd injunction ringing in Lorna's ears.

She held the receiver in her hand for a long time, staring at it, as if trying to conjure up a vision of John's face; and of his eyes. She felt quite sure that he was deeply worried, even though he had tried to keep it from her, and gradually fear took possession of her. She did not start to telephone Toby Pleydell, but pushed the bed-clothes back, put on her dressing-gown, and went across to the dressing-table, mechanically running a comb

through her long hair, not noticing the strands of grey.
How often had she sat doing that with John standing
just behind her? She could judge from his expression the
moment when he was going to slide his arms round her,
when his hands were going to cup her breasts, when he
would make her turn to look at him, and kiss him.

Now, the mirror was empty; dull.

She felt the stirring of panic, and it was useless to tell
herself that there was no need. She felt her breath coming
quick and short. Her grip on the comb tightened. But
she did not move.

The police must feel sure of themselves—that was a
fact she had to accept, and it made the situation
worse.

They had found something at Quinns . . .

It wouldn't be the first time if John had stored jewels
for someone else, knowing they had been stolen. All his
life he had taken chances, often desperate chances. Sometimes, in the early days before their marriage, he had
actually stolen precious stones, and in those days she had
fooled herself that it was a good thing to steal from the
rich to give to the poor. She had put that idea aside long
before he had. Yet the past too often loomed over them to
threaten today's happiness. And the old days of the
Baron had never really been buried. When he had told
her about Rebecca Blest, there had been a gleam in his
eyes and a ring in his voice which had betrayed a lively
interest in the mystery. But for that, he would never have
taken the trouble to go to the girl's home.

Had she taken him fake jewels?

The question was firm in Lorna's mind almost before
she realised its significance. If she herself began to wonder
if he had told the truth, was it surprising that the police
had doubts? She hated herself for the question, yet once
it was there, its importance grew and grew. Why had
John gone to see the girl? Why hadn't he waited until she
returned to him? It was easy to understand him offering
more than the jewels were worth—that was a character-

istic gesture. But what had made him take that extra trouble?

Did anyone else know why? Larraby, for instance?

Lorna turned away from the mirror, got up and went to the telephone. It was natural to turn to Josh in moments of difficulty, for the old man was not only wise but wholly reliable. He was probably asleep, but was used to being disturbed by night.

She dialled his number.

The ringing sound went on and on. For the first half minute she was not surprised; then she began to worry. If Josh were in, he would surely have heard the bell by now, no matter how soundly he had been sleeping. The bell kept on ringing. Brrr-brrr; brrr-brrr. Why didn't he answer? Wasn't he at home? And if he wasn't, why not?

Why should old Josh be out after midnight?

Brrr-brrr; brrr-brrr.

After a long while, she put the receiver down very slowly, and began to dress. She wanted to see Josh Larraby, and if he had run into trouble of any kind, she must tell the police at once.

11

QUESTIONS

MANNERING felt the gaze of the policeman and the plain-clothes men at Scotland Yard as he was taken up the wide stairs towards Bristow's office. He doubted whether any of these men knew exactly what had happened, but rumour of his arrest would have spread by now, and would be a sensation at the Yard. One of their own consultants, one of the most respected men in the jewellery and antique trade, here under a serious charge. Men he knew slightly stared at him, some openly, some covertly. A sergeant on duty at the reception hall, whom he knew well, ignored him. Ingleby wore an expression of almost blissful satisfaction as he led the way, and stopped at a door marked: *Waiting Room.* He opened it, looked inside, and said to the sergeant who had come with him—the man with the snort:

"Wait here with him, Joe."

"Right."

Ingleby moved away, and as he went out of the room, Mannering called quietly:

"Ingleby."

Ingleby stopped. "Well?"

"Why the hate?" demanded Mannering.

"I don't know what you're talking about."

"If you'd caught a murderer you'd been after for years, you couldn't be more pleased with yourself."

Ingleby said: "Couldn't I?" He hesitated, then came back into the room, closed the door, looked Mannering up and down, and said evenly:

"All right, Mannering, I'll tell you why I hate your guts. You've been a consultant at the Yard for as many years as I can remember. If there was one man in London

I thought I could trust, it was you. I recommended you to anyone who wanted a genuine valuation for jewels. I've argued with a dozen of my colleagues over you— I've claimed that you were the one man who was incapable of handling stolen jewels. And most of them agreed with me. I shouldn't think there was a jewel merchant in London more trusted by the Yard, and by the Divisions. Until a few days ago, I was just a mug, like the rest. Then I began to hear these rumours, and we got the reports that you'd been handling Rett Laker's jewels."

Ingleby stopped, moistening his lips and giving the impression that he did not quite know how to go on. The sergeant was staring at his superior officer now, not at Mannering. Ingleby's eyes showed a cold light, and his voice was hard when he went on:

"Rett Laker committed worse than murder when he got those jewels. One of his victims was crippled for life, and a woman was so badly injured that she's never been right in the head since. I hated Laker and men like him as much as I respected you, and when I knew you'd been handling that kind of filthy jewellery—"

Ingleby broke off.

After a long pause, Mannering said: "Thanks for that, anyhow. Just get one thing into your head, will you? I had never seen those jewels until tonight."

Ingleby turned on his heel.

Mannering heard the door close with a snap, then took out cigarettes, lit one, remembered the sergeant, and offered him one; the man shook his head. Mannering had a feeling that the sergeant was beginning to wonder if there could be anything in his, Mannering's, insistence, but he was not left to wonder. Ingleby came back, and said gruffly:

"Superintendent Bristow is ready to see you."

"Now we might get somewhere," Mannering said, but that was as much to raise his own spirits as in hope.

In a way, Bill Bristow was as familiar as Larraby to

Mannering, and at the Yard he was a kind of father figure.
Now he sat behind his tidy pedestal desk in a big room
with the windows overlooking the Thames. Lights shone
on the dark water from Westminster Bridge, car lights
sped like moving diamonds over the bridge and on the
far side of the river. Immediately beneath the window, on
the Embankment, there was a haze of light, and the
buzzing of moving cars. Mannering was almost as familiar
with this as with Bristow. It was many, many years since
he had stepped into this office and not been greeted with a
smile, a 'hallo John', and a handshake. Now, Bristow sat
in his chair, stony-faced, and Mannering stood in front
of him, with Ingleby on one side.

"Well, Mr. Mannering."

"*Et tu*, Bristow?" Mannering murmured. "Mind if I
sit down?" He pulled a chair closer to him, half-prepared
for Bristow to say no; but Bristow made no comment, and
Mannering sat down. "Bill," he went on, "I wouldn't
expect Ingleby to take any notice of this, so I saved it
up for you."

"Saved what up?"

"I'm worried about Josh Larraby."

"Why?"

"Because he was the only man who might have got
into the strong-room tonight."

Bristow said, slowly, heavily, disgustedly: "My God,
you have reached bottom, haven't you?"

Mannering's great effort to be composed, the sense of
relief that he had felt at seeing Bristow, the feeling that
this situation would not become too desperate, all
vanished. There was something in Bristow's expression
which he feared, and even dreaded; some implication in
that "My God, you have reached bottom, haven't you?"
which seemed to tell of disgust. Bristow's eyes were very
bright and steady, but there was no hint of a smile or of
friendliness—or of goodwill.

Mannering said sharply: "What are you driving at?"

"You know as well as I do," Bristow said, coldly. "I

thought that if you were ever caught red-handed you would have the guts to take what was coming to you, not use Larraby as a scapegoat. Don't you think that old man's had enough trouble? Do you think he would risk going inside again?" Bristow leaned forward, and went on with deliberate emphasis: "Or is this the price you've extracted from him? For lifting him out of poverty and giving him a chance, he must cover up for you if you ever got caught."

Mannering said: "So *I've* sunk low." He fought back his resentment, returned Bristow's cold gaze, and went on: "I would like my solicitor, at once."

"I asked you a question."

"I heard it," said Mannering. "And I want my solicitor here, because I've finished talking to you. If you want the situation to be legal and formal, that's all right with me. But when the case is over, blame yourself for any harm that comes of it. If Larraby's hurt, if he's dead, remind yourself that you and your stooges were so busy following false trails that you didn't give a damn about his danger."

"What danger?"

"You can't be that dumb."

"I don't want rudeness, and—"

"You don't want rudeness!" cried Mannering. Now he was beginning to act his part; he had needled Bristow, and that might put an edge on to Bristow's hostility. "Forget what you want. Just try to get it into your head that Larraby was the only man, beside me, who could have got into my strong-room tonight, and nothing in the world would have made him do it unless he was under threat. I've always told him to give in if he came up against an emergency with his life at stake—and his life must have been at stake for him to allow anyone into Quinns to plant those jewels. Find Josh, and you stand half a chance of discovering what happened. You also stand a chance of finding him with his head bashed in, like the other victims of this killer. Put out a call for Josh Larraby, and get a move on."

Bristow hesitated, then put his right hand on the

telephone. He lifted it, said: "*Information*," and waited. Then he went on: "George, I want a general call out for a man named Josh Larraby, who . . . Yes, that's right, Mannering's manager at Quinns. I'll go to his flat, you go to his friends, and pick him up wherever he is. If you can't find him quickly, try the hospitals and casualty wards. Is that clear?"

After a pause, Bristow rang off.

Mannering said heavily: "Thanks."

"Mannering," Bristow said, relaxing a little, "why don't you stop trying to fool us? I've put out a call for Larraby because there's a ten per cent chance that you're right, but there's a ninety per cent chance that you're trying to mislead us. That girl brought you the real jewels this afternoon, and you had your own reasons for saying they were false. What were they?"

"Those jewels were false."

"The moment I heard that they'd been found at Quinns, I went to Notting Hill, and talked to the Blest girl myself," said Bristow. "She was glad of a chance to talk—she'd refused to have a sedative, and was desperately anxious to have something to do. She said that she felt absolutely sure that she brought you the real jewels, and was astounded when she heard that they were false. She also said that no one else at Quinns saw those jewels, so no one could corroborate your story that they were false. Now, let's have the truth: why did you lie to her? Were you under some kind of pressure?"

"No, Bill," Mannering said. "I didn't lie to her."

"You're not seriously insisting that someone broke into Quinns, took away some fake jewels worth a few hundred pounds, and left thirty or forty thousand pounds worth of genuine jewellery in their place?"

"That's exactly what happened." Mannering was almost tired of saying it.

"I don't believe you."

"Nor do I," muttered Ingleby.

"Supposing I have my solicitor now," said Mannering.

Bristow said: "As a matter of fact, Mannering, I telephoned your friend Pleydell after you had been charged. I knew that he was due in court two days ago, and hadn't appeared, so he was either out of the country, or ill. He's out of the country. He and his wife flew at short notice to the United States three days ago, over some complicated estate business, and are likely to be away for a month. His partners can act for you, of course, if you want them."

Mannering echoed: "Partners." In a disturbing way everything seemed to be working against him, and this last was in some ways the worst blow. Pleydell knew something of his past; Pleydell could deal with the police much better than anyone else. Each of his partners was strange to Mannering's career and to his business. It would be almost impossible to brief another man quickly and fully; it would be better in some ways to act for himself.

"Well?" Bristow demanded.

Mannering said: "I'll think about it. Why did you telephone?"

"I wanted to know what I would be up against," Bristow said. "But even Pleydell couldn't have got you home tonight. The police court hearing will be fairly easy in the morning. If you need anything, they'll get it for you at Cannon Row." He stood up. "And if I hear any news of Larraby, I'll let you know."

"Just tell me whether he's alive."

"You seem pretty sure that he's in danger," Ingleby interpolated, out of the blue. "That looks damned odd to me."

"Looks *what*?"

Bristow was momentarily unable to meet Mannering's eyes as he said:

"Ingleby's suggesting that if Larraby's been attacked you might have as good a motive as anyone to attack him —a dead Larraby couldn't betray you, could he?"

"Ah," said Mannering. After a long pause, he added:

"No, he couldn't, could he? Bill, answer me this: why are you pretending to be so sure that you know what you're doing? You're the one man at the Yard who ought to know that there can't be any truth in this. I can understand Ingleby being doubtful, and I know all about the other men, but you—"

He broke off.

Bristow looked out of the window, as if he could not meet Mannering's gaze at all, and he leaned his hand heavily on the desk. A big truck roared past, rattling the windows. Bristow had a cigarette burning very low between his lips, and the thick grey smoke was coiling about his neatly trimmed moustache.

He said: "When you agreed to handle the Rett Laker jewels, you went too far. I suppose you thought that the robbery was too old for anyone to be interested in today, but you made a mistake. A big mistake. We believed that Laker would lead us to the jewels soon after he came out. We were watching him closely. The only people with whom he had close associations after his release were his relations, including Samuel Blest and his daughter, Rebecca. We can't be sure whom he talked to by telephone, and occasionally he evaded our men watching him, but we have no reason to believe that he was in touch with anybody who had facilities for selling jewels—except you, at Quinns."

Mannering exclaimed: "Quinns? What makes you think that he was in touch with Quinns?"

"No, dammit!" exclaimed Ingleby, as if he were out of patience.

Bristow said, very precisely: "He was in and out of Quinns frequently. You must know it."

"I don't know anyone called Laker," Mannering answered, but his voice had gone husky.

"Are you positive?"

"Yes." Mannering replied. After a moment, he went on: "So he came to me under an assumed name. I'd never seen him to my knowledge." He thought swiftly of callers whom he had not known until recently. One possibility was a man named Klein, but he wanted to be sure before he said so. "If I'd known—" He broke off, moistening his lips, feeling bitter towards Bristow, the Yard, everyone even remotely involved. Bristow could have told him that an ex-jewel thief was a regular visitor to Quinns. The Bristow of a few months ago would have telephoned him and said: "Oi, John, what's this all about?" But Bristow had allowed Laker's visits to pass without comment. It was now clear that he and Ingleby felt sure that Mannering had known the identity of his visitor.

Even if he had suspected this man Klein, the name Laker would have meant nothing to him. The case must have been heard when he had been away; he could not recall anything about it.

Could the Yard be blamed for refusing to believe that he, the owner of Quinns, the man with such a great knowledge of precious stones, was unaware of such a man's identity?

The awful problem would be to convince the police, the magistrate, even the judge.

Would it really come to trial?

For the first time, Mannering was beginning to fear that there was no way to prevent it.

"I don't think we're going to get any further by talking about it," Bristow said. "Chief Inspector, take Mr. Mannering across to Cannon Row. I've laid everything on."

"Right, sir." Ingleby was still dour.

Mannering said: "Don't forget to look for Larraby," and turned to go with Ingleby.

The sergeant who had been with him at Quinns was waiting outside, and they walked briskly back the way they had come. Doors were open now, although most had been closed when they had come in. Mannering saw faces at the doorways; plainclothes men, sergeants, inspectors, uniformed officers, all anxious to catch a glimpse of him. He felt as if his hands were fastened with invisible handcuffs; it was like being led out to the stocks.

He went down in the lift; five men were waiting in the passage when he stepped out, Ingleby in the lead, the sergeant just behind. He walked down the wide stone steps between them, and could not have felt more conspicuous if there had been a chain round his neck. Then he saw a man come walking briskly up, holding something at his side. It wasn't until the man reached the foot of the steps that he put a camera to his eyes, cried: "Hold it!" and pressed. Vivid light flashed. Mannering was momentarily blinded. Ingleby cried out: "Stop him!" The photographer, knowing what to expect, made a rush for the gates, and only half-hearted attempts were made to prevent him from getting out.

When Mannering sat on the bed in the cell at Cannon Row, the light from that flash bulb seemed to glisten on the retina of his eyes, still dazzling him. He kept telling himself that he must get some rest, or he would be unable to cope in the morning, but there were too many things on his mind. The dead Samuel Blest; the injured man reeling against the wall; Larraby; the false jewels which had become real; the girl, the motor-cyclist, Lorna—and the fact that the ex-jewel thief, Laker, had been coming in and out of Quinns, without his knowledge.

Surely someone at the shop had recognised him— Larraby must have, if no one else. He had been out of England, perhaps, but Larraby hadn't; there was no reason to believe that Larraby had not known about Rett Laker.

It kept coming back to Larraby.

12

BLACKER STILL

LORNA kept her finger on the bell push outside Larraby's little flat, and could hear the ringing sound inside, but nothing else. Only now and again did a car pass. Once she heard some people laughing and giggling, not far away; happy people did not seem part of this chill night. She had been here for several minutes, the cold creeping into her, still alarmed by all that was happening. Why wasn't Josh here? Why didn't he answer?

She stopped ringing, almost decided to give up, and then tried once again. As the ringing sound came, she heard a car engine approaching at speed, then heard it change gear. Headlamps were switched on suddenly, and the car swung round the corner into the mews, shining on her, casting her shadow black against the wall. She turned round, wondering if this could be Larraby in a taxi, but it wasn't a taxi. The car stopped a few yards away from her, a door opened almost as soon as the wheels stopped moving, and the driver jumped out and opened the back door. The reflected light from the headlamps shone on Bill Bristow.

Lorna exclaimed: "Bill!" and turned and stepped towards him. She sensed his reserve before she reached him, and it did nothing to ease her anxiety about John. But this man was an old friend, an old family friend; Bristow had done more to help John over the years than anyone.

"Good evening, Mrs. Mannering," Bristow said. His tone was obviously calculated to establish a mood of formality. "May I ask what you're doing here?"

Lorna said: "I want to talk to Josh Larraby. Is John—?" she broke off.

"I'm sorry that it was necessary to detain Mr. Mannering," Bristow said. "Isn't Larraby in?"

"I can't get any reply."

"Have you a key?"

"No," Lorna said. "No, but John has."

Bristow said: "If Mr. Mannering has a key, perhaps it's one of these." He took a bunch of keys out of his pocket; they made a jingling sound. Lorna, recognising the large key-ring as John's, knew that the police had taken his keys. She gulped down a lump in her throat, as Bristow asked: "Would you recognise it?"

"No."

"Try the door with these, please," Bristow said to the man who had jumped out of the car; and stood watching as he obeyed. Lorna stared at the door and the pale hand in the light from the car's headlamps. Bristow didn't speak. Key after key scraped against the metal of the keyhole, but didn't go into the hole itself. At last the man said: "Ah, that's it," and after a moment the key turned in the lock, and the man pushed the door wide open. "Shall I lead the way, sir?"

"Yes. Are you coming, Mrs. Mannering?"

Lorna answered "Yes", in a low-pitched voice, and followed Bristow into the narrow hall. She heard Bristow tread on something which made a grating sound, and he looked down; he appeared to have trodden on a piece of glass. He looked round, but saw nothing else, and went in the wake of the first man. Lorna had visited here occasionally, and she knew that it would take only a minute to search. If Larraby were here—

"There he is!" exclaimed the Yard man.

"He's *here*?" Bristow sounded startled.

"Sleeping like a log," the other Yard man declared, and went further into Larraby's bedroom. Lorna could hardly believe that Josh was in the room. She told herself almost wildly that it must be a mistake; it must be someone else. She made herself step after Bristow, looked over his shoulder, and saw Larraby lying on his side.

She did not know that he was lying in exactly the same position as Samuel Blest had been when he was found dead.

Larraby didn't appear to be hurt, and there could be no mistaking his snow-white hair. The two men and Lorna stared down at the back of his head, the one arm over the bedclothes with the pyjama sleeve rucked up to the elbow in an almost child-like attitude of repose.

Next to the bed was a small table with a telephone on it; the telephone should have woken him.

"Larraby!" Bristow spoke sharply, but the old man did not stir. "Larraby!" The other Yard man went forward and shook Larraby's shoulder. His head moved to and fro, but he made no sound or movement of his own accord. Chilled and dismayed by all that had happened, Lorna felt that she wanted to shout at the manager of Quinns. Then quite suddenly new fear stabbed into her, and she cried:

"Josh!"

She pushed past Bristow, reached the bed, called "Josh!" again, bent down, and turned Larraby's head. She raised it a little, and it lolled back. His eyes were closed and his mouth slack.

"No," Lorna said in a choking whisper. "He can't be dead. No!"

"Let me see, Mrs. Mannering," Bristow said brusquely. Tension showed in his voice, and in the way he moved. The other man rounded the bed, while Bristow took Larraby's wrist, and felt for the pulse. Lorna stared at the policeman's lean, strong hand, and at Larraby's pale, veined one, with the very thin fingers and beautifully shaped nails, and for a few seconds she felt as if she could not breathe. Now she wanted to scream for a different reason. Why didn't Bristow say something? Why didn't—?

"He's alive," Bristow told her at last, "but the pulse is very slow." As if to himself, he muttered: "It seems like some kind of drug." He let Larraby's arm fall, and said: "Telephone for a doctor and an ambulance." As the

other man picked up the receiver, Bristow pulled back
one of Larraby's eyelids, showing the white of the eye
vividly, unpleasantly. The slackness of his body seemed to
give Bristow the lie; no one could have looked more dead.
"Not a pin point," Bristow observed, in a matter-of-fact
voice. "It isn't one of the morphine drugs. He could just
have made sure of a night's sleep." Obviously Bristow
didn't believe that. "We'll look after him, Mrs. Mannering. You needn't worry about that."

Lorna said: "You've got to."

"We will," repeated Bristow, and then asked in the
same quiet voice: "Is John in any financial difficulties?"

Lorna stared.

"No, of course not."

"Are you sure?"

"I'm quite sure. What makes you ask— ?" Lorna broke
off, in sudden understanding.

Bristow said: "Something must explain what's going on.
Do you remember having met a man named Rett Laker?"

"No," said Lorna, tautly.

Bristow shook his head, slowly. Lorna had the impression that he hated the situation and what he had to
say; there was no doubt of his seriousness.

"John most certainly did. There isn't any possible doubt
about it. Laker visited the shop frequently—until three
weeks ago, when he died."

"I don't believe it."

"Over the period concerned, at least eight detective
officers can testify that it's true," Bristow declared, and
put a hand on her arm. "Lorna, what's the trouble? How
bad is it?"

The gentleness of his voice, the friendliness of his
manner after the earlier aloofness, the familiarity of his
touch upon her arm, all combined to make her feel sure
that he was deeply concerned, and the doubt which had
come to her mind earlier flared up again. John *knew*
Laker, and yet had denied it absolutely. Bristow wouldn't
make such a statement unless he were quite sure of

himself. If John had lied about Laker, what else had he kept from her? Was he in some kind of serious financial trouble, enough to explain him taking desperate chances?

Suddenly, angrily, she thought: No! Bristow's trying to trick me.

"Lorna—"

"The only trouble is that he tried to help this girl this afternoon."

"You really mustn't deceive yourself," Bristow insisted. Although he released her arm, his voice and manner were still gentle. "It's much more serious than that—and it began a lot earlier than this afternoon. Lorna, my dear, if you want my advice, and I give it to you as a friend, persuade John to tell us what is happening. He wouldn't take part in an affair like this without good reason. It's possible that he's being forced into it, and daren't—"

"It isn't possible, and he knows nothing more than he's told us," Lorna said. "And I certainly don't want your advice." She looked down at Larraby, seeing that his body was as limp as ever, and wondered what secrets were hidden inside that white head. "Look after Josh," she said huskily, and turned and went out of the room. Bristow and the other man stared after her, then Bristow followed her to the passage, but she was already at the front door, and going out.

"Lorna!" Bristow called, but she ignored him and stepped down into the cobbled yard. The driver of the police car was standing by it, and Bristow's shadow was thrown from the doorway. The driver moved, as if he meant to impede Lorna, then stopped as Bristow called more formally:

"This won't help you or your husband, Mrs. Mannering."

Lorna walked towards the mouth of the mews, her shoulders back, her head high. She knew that both men were staring after her, but did not look round. A clock struck one, not far away; was that one o'clock or half-past twelve? It mattered, because there was still something she needed to do, and she did not know whether or not it was too late. She wanted to go and see the Blest girl. *Blest!* She walked towards Berkeley Square, and saw two taxis with their *For Hire* signs lit up, waiting near a night club which had an obscure little doorway. She went to the first.

"I want to go as far as Notting Hill," she said. "And back after half an hour or so."

"Anywhere you like, lady."

Lorna sat back in the taxi, playing with the clasp of her handbag. Her head was aching, and her mouth was dry, but she lit a cigarette, and stared at the road in front of the driver, trying to picture John in a cell, trying to reconcile everything she knew with the doubts which would not vanish from her mind. The worst blow was the statement that John had known Laker. If he had, why hadn't he told her so? Why lie to her? Didn't he know that he could trust her?

Suddenly, she thought: *Tom will know!* She leaned forward and tapped at the driver's window, and he turned his head. "Will you go to Meyrick Street, Hammersmith, first, please—number 17."

"Okay, lady." The driver certainly meant to oblige.

Tom Wainwright came down from his bedroom, five minutes after Lorna had called at the house, and his mother hovered in the background, as if to make sure that she learned exactly what a late call like this was about. Tom's dark hair was standing up like quills on one side of his head; he looked sleepy and his grey-green eyes were huge. He wore bright pink pyjamas with a grey dressing-gown loosely tied round his lean body.

He listened . . .

"No, Mrs. Mannering. I didn't know anyone named Laker, and no one of that name came and asked for Mr. Mannering. But he makes some appointments for himself, you know, and I've often known people refuse to give their names."

"How many, recently?" asked Lorna; and when Tom

rubbed the end of his nose as if trying to rouse himself properly, she went on: "This man came out of prison a year ago, and died about three weeks ago, so it would be someone who didn't visit the shop until last year, and stopped coming some time last month. Does that help?"

"I'll do some hard thinking," Tom said. "Mr. Larraby would know, but—"

Lorna told him what had happened to Larraby.

"I don't like the sound of that," Tom said. He was a naïve young man in some ways, likeable, loyal and knowledgeable, but not highly intelligent. No one could have been more willing. "Look here, Mrs. Mannering, wait five minutes and I'll put some clothes on, and then come with you. We need all hands at the pump for this, don't we?" When Lorna didn't speak, he went on: "Who are you going to see next?"

"Rebecca Blest," Lorna said. "John told me where to find her. Thank you, Tom. Please hurry."

13

PHOTOGRAPH

"No, I wasn't asleep," said Rebecca Blest. Her eyes were bright and huge, as if she badly needed sleep, and her young body seemed tense. She looked very young, and really pretty in a dressing-gown a pale shade of pink. She had run a comb through her hair and put on powder, but no lipstick or rouge, and received them in the living-room of the flat. "I haven't been able to sleep, and I'm quite all right, really—the girl from the flat downstairs is staying with me, but I'm all right." She spoke tiredly, mechanically. "I'm sorry to hear that Mr. Mannering is in this trouble, but—"

She broke off.

"Miss Blest, I hate trying to make you answer questions now, but it is very urgent," Lorna said. "Will you try to help?"

"If I can."

"Had you ever heard your uncle, Rett Laker, talk about my husband?"

"No, I haven't."

"Or did your father talk about him?"

"Not until yesterday, when I telephoned Sothebys and asked advice about the jewels. A man there sent us to Quinns and Mr. Mannering."

There would be no useful lead from a man at Sothebys, Lorna knew; if the Blests had been recommended to Quinns by someone else, it might have been significant, but Sothebys were as solid and reputable as the Bank of England.

"Do you know if your father ever went to Quinns?"

"Of course he didn't," the girl answered. "He had never heard of the shop before." She didn't say so, but obviously she was beginning to wonder where these questions were leading. Now that she was talking, she seemed to become tired, and droop.

There was a movement at the door, and a thin girl in her late teens appeared, brown hair bedraggled, wearing a shabby dressing-gown. She looked at Lorna resentfully.

"You shouldn't make her talk like this. She ought to be asleep."

"Yes, I know," Lorna said. "And I'm really sorry." She felt desperate. "Miss Blest, have you a photograph of your uncle?"

"Oh, yes. It's all right, Ruth," Rebecca added. "I don't mind."

"You *have*?" exclaimed Lorna.

"It's not a very good one," Rebecca went on hurriedly. "I bought a new camera a few weeks ago, and took a picture of my uncle and my father—my father's last birthday. He was sixty-three. Sixty-three," she repeated, huskily, and turned away. She went across to a bureau, pulling the drawer open so vigorously that it nearly came right out.

"You shouldn't worry her," insisted Ruth Ashton. "It's not fair."

"I won't be a minute," Lorna promised, and she approached Rebecca as the girl turned round with the photograph in her hand. Tom came forward as eagerly as Lorna. Rebecca held out the photograph. It was an enlargement of a snapshot, showing two men standing quite close together, one looking frail and old, the other taller, stockier, heartier. Tom twisted his head round so that he could see properly, and exclaimed:

"I know *him*." Excitement made his voice shrill. "He was often in the shop!" He pointed to the stockier-looking man on the right of the photograph. "But his name wasn't Laker, he said that it was Klein. Jacob Klein. He saw Mr. Mannering several times."

After a long pause, the skinny girl from downstairs said sourly:

"Well, if you've got what you wanted, perhaps you'll leave Rebecca in peace. If you don't, I'm going to fetch my father."

"It's all right, Ruth," Rebecca Blest said. "I can see that Mrs. Mannering's worried, but—that was my uncle."

Tom asked with unexpected shrewdness: "Did you know him before he went to prison?"

"Oh, yes."

"And you're sure it was the same man?"

"Of course I'm sure," replied Rebecca. "You couldn't mistake him. There's another photograph of him taken about fifteen years ago; you can see for yourself." She turned round to the bureau again, took out a photograph album, flipped over the pages, and then pointed to a man who was obviously the same one, although much younger. "But why should he use a false name?"

"We'll find out," Lorna said, quietly. "Thank you very much, Miss Blest. If there is anything at all I can do to help, you'll tell me, won't you?"

"But there isn't anything," Rebecca said. "I don't see that anybody can do anything."

As she spoke, she looked up, for there was a thump of footsteps. A thickset man appeared, with trousers over his pyjamas, and with a rather truculent manner.

"Now what is all this? Eh? What's up, Ruth?"

"Dad, they won't leave Becky alone!" the girl from downstairs exclaimed. "It's not fair, they keep on at her."

"Who are you, and what's this all about?" the man demanded, brusquely.

"It's all right, Mr. Ashton," Rebecca insisted. "I really don't mind, honestly I don't."

But it was obviously time for Lorna to go.

.   .   .   .   .

The taxi bowled along the empty road from Notting Hill Gate and towards Kensington, turned to the right, and headed for Chelsea. Tom was sitting in a corner, smoking a cigarette, taking furtive glances at Lorna as the car passed beneath street lamps. There was no traffic about, and London had a curious eeriness.

It was after three o'clock; three clocks hanging outside lighted shop windows all showed that, though differing from one another by as much as ten minutes. Tom had insisted on coming to the Chelsea flat, and Lorna hadn't had the heart to tell him not to; in any case, it would be good to have him at hand. Her head was aching more than ever, and fear was deep in her. She could not tell whether the new identity of the man Laker was important at all.

Klein.

So far as Tom knew, the man calling himself Klein had been a dealer from Nairobi, opening an account with Mannering at Quinns, but had not discussed business with anyone else at the shop. Klein had started coming four months ago, saying that he was in England for a few months; when he had stopped coming, a month ago, Tom had assumed he had gone back to Nairobi.

The simple, inescapable fact was that John had seen and talked to the man. All the assistants at the shop would now be able to testify to that, as well as Bristow's detectives.

Could John have been deceived?

Could he really have been unaware of 'Klein's' true identity?

Even if he had been, would it ever be possible to convince the police of that?

Now that they were nearing Chelsea, Lorna began to think about Larraby again, and was eager to find out if there was any news. The taxi turned into Green Street, where two men sat in a car half-way along the road; she had no doubt that they were watching the flat. There was a uniformed constable inside the ground floor hall, and he let them in. He was civil enough.

They went up in the lift. Lorna was aware of Tom staring at her, as if anxiously; she probably looked washed out. She took out her key and handed it to him, and he

opened the door and stood aside for her to go in. The
first surprise was to find the hall light on; the next was the
figure of Chittering of the *Daily Globe*, rising from a chair
in the study, the door of which was wide open. He came
forward, hands outstretched: a thin man in the late
thirties who looked no more than twenty-five, a little
reminiscent of Larraby to look at, with curly fair hair
and a round, impudent kind of face. There was nothing
cheeky about his expression now, and his blue eyes were
troubled.

"Hallo, Lorna." He took her hands. "I can't tell you
how sorry I am about this."

"I know you must be," Lorna said. She let him squeeze
her hands, freed herself, took her hat off, and put it on a
table in the hall. "Is there any news?" She was afraid of
what the answer would be, and added huskily: "About
Josh, I mean."

"He's at St. George's Hospital," Chittering told her. "I
couldn't get much out of the police, but one of our chaps
knows a nurse there, on night duty, and she says it looks
like a case of an overdose of some sleeping pills—barbitu-
rates of a kind." He rubbed his chin. "Crazy, of course,
but the hospital authorities seem to take it for granted that
it was attempted suicide. So do the police."

"Suicide—Josh Larraby? They're crazy!" Tom almost
spluttered.

"Suicide is what it seems like," Chittering said. He
lit a cigarette. "Lorna, you look as if you could do with a
pick-me-up. Going to have a drink, or some coffee? I got
Ethel to put some on, and it's been percolating for half
an hour. What a girl she is for sleep!" he added, breezily.
"She could hardly keep awake long enough to let me in,
and when she opened the door she thought I was a policeman. She does not love policemen!" Chittering was trying
to introduce a more cheerful note into the atmosphere,
and half-succeeding.

He led the way into the kitchen, where the coffee
percolator bubbled and muttered. Cups were on a tray,

with cream, sugar, biscuits, butter, and some cheese.
Lorna sat on Ethel's chair, Chittering leaned against the
sink, Tom against the larder door, as they all sipped
coffee. "Er—the really bad news sent me here," Chittering
added. "I'd heard that John was on a charge, and went
to the Yard to find out what it was all about. Some
beggar got a picture, by the way, and nothing would
stop my Editor from using it. Don't blame me. He—"

"The really bad news?" Lorna made herself ask.

"Yes," said Chittering, gently. "Very nasty, indeed,
I'm afraid. The man Farmer died without recovering
consciousness. So it is murder. And from what I could
piece together from bits and pieces I was told at the Yard,
there seems a reasonable chance that they think John hit
him while he was here."

Lorna said: "Oh, dear God."

"They're going crazy!" gasped Tom.

"That's the word," declared Chittering. He put his cup
down in the sink, turned and stared straight at Lorna,
looking very much older than his years. "But *we* mustn't
go crazy. We've a lot of work to do. Toby Pleydell is out
of England, and John hasn't a lawyer to act for him with
any knowledge of the background. John's under arrest on
a charge of being in possession of stolen goods, but now
that Farmer's dead, the charge might be changed to one
of murder."

Lorna caught her breath.

"No use blinking at the facts," Chittering went on
grimly. "If the charge is being in possession of stolen
goods, and John asked for bail, he would probably get
it—he could put up any amount as surety, and could get
plenty of others to stand for him, too. But there's no chance
of bail on a murder charge, and from what I could gather
at the Yard, that's what they're likely to go for."

"Murder!" Tom said; he almost choked. "My God, it
looks as if they're doing anything to break Mr. Mannering!
And after all he's done to help—"

"More likely because of all he's done to help," Chittering suggested. "It's no use blinking at facts, and the fact is that John has often solved cases which the Yard couldn't—or at least, which they didn't. Even though he's been a consultant on special inquiries concerning precious stones, a lot of the Yard men have resented it—amateurs always run into trouble at the Yard, sooner or later. There's a lot of bitterness, a feeling that a man they've trusted, one of the few they've worked with, has been hiding behind them as a cover in order to pull off crime after crime. It's no use calling them bloody fools, either— that's what they believe, or what a lot of them believe. The pressure on the Assistant Commissioner to make it a murder charge will be so great I doubt if he'll be able to resist it."

.   .   .   .

The Assistant Commissioner for Crime looked at the man from the solicitor's office and at the man from the Public Prosecutor's office, then down at the recommendations in front of him, and asked:

"What do you think, Bristow?"

"If we want to keep Mannering in custody, it's got to be the murder charge," Bristow said. "If we put him up on the other, he'll get bail. This is a case where it's easier to believe that the prisoner would commit murder than to believe that he would traffic in stolen goods. Remember, Mannering's had years of glamour treatment from the Press, and he's a kind of public hero in the eyes of a lot of people. He'll get a lot of sympathy on the receiving charge, but none if he's accused of murder."

"Never mind what public sympathy he'll get," said the Assistant Commissioner. "If he were released on bail, could we keep tabs on him?"

"If he's really frightened, I think he could find a way to get out of the country," Bristow said. He was speaking very precisely. "He buys and sells all over the world, and has bank accounts in a dozen different countries. I don't think we could keep him in England, and I don't think we could find him easily."

"So you think the murder charge is the right one."

Bristow said gruffly: "I hate the idea of it. On the one hand there's the evidence, and I think we could make it pretty convincing in court. On the other hand, there's my knowledge of Mannering. I could easily believe that he was holding these jewels for some third party, and taking a chance of getting into trouble himself. I can't believe that he would commit murder." Bristow gave a strained laugh. "I called Cannon Row before coming in here, and checked. Mannering was awake until about half-past one, and then he seemed to have gone to sleep; he was still sleeping at eight o'clock. Some people would say that was a sign of an easy conscience."

"Or of a hardened criminal," said the Public Prosecutor's man. "I don't think there's any question: Mannering should be charged with murder, and you should ask for the usual eight-day remand. That will give you time to get inquiries under way. This man Larraby should have recovered by then, and be ready to talk. I know Mannering is an old friend of yours, Bristow—that fact ought to make you feel even more angry about this."

Bristow said: "Should it?"

"We'll make the charge murder," insisted the Assistant Commissioner.

14

REMAND

". . . and in accordance with the indications which I saw at the apartment on the top floor of 28, Green Street, Chelsea, I came to the conclusion that the accused had been the only person in a position to carry out the assault upon the then injured man who has since died," deposed Ingleby. "Subsequently I took the accused into custody on a less serious charge and later was advised of the death of the man assaulted. I thereupon charged the accused with the wilful murder of Stanley James Farmer, and he replied that he was not guilty. It is the request of the police that the accused be remanded in custody while full inquiries can be made."

Ingleby stopped.

Mannering stood in the dock above the crowded court, trying not to meet Lorna's eyes too often. Even across the court he could see that they were red-rimmed, and had dark patches under them; she hadn't had much sleep. Tom was with her. Chittering was in the reporters' benches, which were so crowded that it was almost impossible for them to make notes. The rest of the court was jammed tight with people. The only space was on the bench itself, where the magistrate sat in solitary state, and immediately below him, where his clerk was busy writing the evidence of arrest.

The magistrate, Mr. McKenzie-James, was a middle-aged benevolent-looking, balding individual who wore pince-nez.

"Is the accused represented?" he inquired.

No one answered, and the clerk looked up, testily.

"*Is* the accused represented?"

"Yes, sir," said Lloyd, a stocky man from Pleydell's

office. Mannering had talked to him for an hour this morning, and at least felt certain that he knew what he was about. "I represent Mr. Mannering, and I would like to assure the court that he has a complete answer to this and in fact to any other charges which have been most unfairly hinted at by the police, and pleads not guilty."

"I see," said McKenzie-James.

"And with your permission, your Honour, I would like to apply for bail in this case. The accused is a highly respected and wholly reputable citizen. He has afforded the police a great deal of assistance in the past and in fact has been responsible for bringing many criminals to justice. Given the opportunity of personally conducting the investigation into this murder it is likely that he will once again be able to find the truth ahead of the authorities. My client is of course fully prepared to offer the highest recognisances and seven persons of the highest reputation are prepared to act as surety for him. He . . ."

"Your Honour," Ingleby said, when Lloyd had finished, "this is the gravest charge which can be made and the police are not satisfied that the accused would stay in the country if allowed out on bail. In any case, he could certainly not be allowed to carry out any kind of investigation which might obstruct the police. We consider a remand in custody is the only safe course."

The magistrate said: "Mr. Lloyd?"

It was a foregone conclusion, Mannering thought grimly. No one could alter the course of events. Lloyd could try, but on a charge like this bail was unthinkable; the application would make a good Press story, that was all.

Lloyd was sweating in the stuffy court. Lorna was watching Lloyd as if she really believed that she could will the magistrate into making the concession. Bristow, who had kept out of the witness box, was sitting with the Public Prosecutor's solicitor, fingering his moustache as if wishing that he could light a cigarette. To Mannering, there was an air of unreality about the whole situation. It was difficult to believe that he was the central figure; as difficult to believe the picture he had been shown in the *Globe*. Between Ingleby and the sergeant, he had looked as if he were being hustled to his cell.

"There is so little positive evidence against my client, who is quite sure that it can be easily established that the dead man received the injuries which afterwards proved fatal before he arrived at the flat in Green Street. My client's special knowledge of such situations is likely to enable him to find the conclusive evidence before the police, and thus save himself from the obloquy of a prolonged period of suspicion. *Any* amount of bail could be met, your Honour."

"I'm quite sure it could," said the magistrate drily. "However, I cannot see that your client could harm himself or his case if he were to pass on any special knowledge which he has to the police—I am quite sure that their only interest is to find out the truth. The accused is remanded in custody for eight days and will appear in this court on the eighth day by which time I trust the police will have finished their inquiries."

"We hope to have them completed, sir," Ingleby said. He gave a satisfied smile. "Thank you, sir."

Lorna was looking across the room at Mannering; smiling. *Smiling.* No one could know what that cost her. Mannering raised a hand to her, and pointed to the door which led to the rooms behind the court. She stood up. Chittering raised his right hand in greeting. Tom muttered something. Lloyd pushed his way through the crowd of officials towards Lorna, obviously to bring her to the back of the court.

Mannering felt the touch of a court warder's hand on his arm—a firm touch, which could tighten, which could be like a steel band. He turned round, slowly. There was a rustle and a clatter of feet on bare boards, as nearly everyone tried to get out. Mannering went down the four steps to the door which was being held open, and stepped into the old, bare-walled passages which led to the police quarters, the magistrates' quarters and the cells. He shivered.

So much had gone wrong, so many things pointed the finger of accusation, that it was almost possible to believe that he could be sent for trial, that he could even be found guilty. He saw Bristow staring at him; Bristow looked away quickly. He was an old *friend*, remember. Why was he behaving as if he thought that there was no serious doubt about Mannering's guilt? Was he putting on an act simply to impress his colleagues, or did he believe the evidence to be overwhelming?

Mannering was led into a small, bare, bleak room, with a barred window. A moment later Lloyd came in, and immediately behind him, Lorna. Mannering's heart leapt as she came, arms outstretched. He held them tightly, drew her to him, could feel the fast beating of her heart, the soft fullness of her breasts, the agitation of her breathing. They stood together without speaking for what seemed a long time, until Lloyd coughed and said drily:

"You have five minutes."

Mannering almost crushed Lorna's hands.

"Yes," he said. "Thanks." He saw Bristow at the doorway, and gave a faint smile. "Thanks for something, Bill."

Bristow closed the door.

"John, my darling," Lorna said in a steady voice. "What do you want us to do?"

That was so right, so exactly right. Mannering raised his hands, as if hopelessly, saw the gleam in Lorna's eyes, could imagine what she was feeling, could even imagine the doubts she had known.

Mannering said: "We've seven clear days, and that should be enough. Bristow told me that Larraby's been drugged but isn't dangerously ill. It's certain that he opened the strong-room under some kind of pressure, and the first thing is to find out why. My guess is that he's been told that if he doesn't keep silent, you'll be in danger, but it's only a guess. The first hope, then, is Josh."

"Yes," said Lorna. "I realise that. John—"

"Mannering," Lloyd said, "did you see a man named Klein, Jacob Klein, at Quinns?"

So it was Klein.

"Yes. A dealer from Nairobi."

"Is this him?" Lloyd produced the snapshot, with that of Samuel Blest hidden by a slip of paper. Mannering studied it for a moment, then looked hard at Lloyd.

"Yes. Why?"

"His name is Laker—or *was* Laker."

Mannering began: "*What*—" and broke off. He stared at the photograph again. The blood in his veins seemed to become colder and colder now that the worst was known. This ex-killer had been to Quinns, often. Who would believe that Mannering had not known his real name?

Lorna said: "Darling," and broke off in her turn. He glanced at her. "Yes," he went on, "I saw him half a dozen times or more. He told me that he was a dealer from Nairobi, and that he had bought a great deal of jewellery from some European and Indian families who wanted money transferred to banks in England—they hadn't felt safe with so much jewellery on their hands." He could picture the man now, with his rather harsh, heavy voice, a man he had not liked particularly, but who had seemed to know a lot about precious stones.

"Did you do any business with this Klein?" asked Lloyd.

"No," said Mannering, slowly. "We didn't get to that stage. He said that he was going to do a big deal, and wanted it all over in one go. He also wanted assurance from me that I had outlets for half a million pounds worth of jewellery, mostly old fashioned—Georgian, Victorian, Edwardian. Once convinced that I had, he haggled over the commission I should have. He—"

Mannering broke off, almost unbelievingly.

"Go on," said Lloyd, heavily.

"He made sure that I had the outlets, and was certain that I could sell half a million pounds worth of jewels to specialised dealers and private collectors. He said that he was anxious to make the deal secretly, so that reports that the British and Asians in Kenya and other parts of Africa were selling out wouldn't get about. It sounded plausible."

"Did you agree to deal with him?"

Mannering said, heavily: "I would have. I asked for the usual references about his integrity, and guarantees that he had the right to sell the jewels. He said he would get them once we'd settled terms. I wanted ten per cent on any sales, he offered five. We didn't reach agreement, and when he didn't turn up again, I thought he'd gone to someone else."

Everything about Klein, *alias* Laker, was vivid in his mind; the rather pale skin, a "prison" skin but not unlike the pallor which some people acquired when living in hot climates; the full lips, the slate grey eyes, the rather wide nostrils. He had not been a handsome man.

Lloyd said: "I can tell you that the jewels Laker stole were worth nearly half a million pounds, so the few you've seen were only a sample. It looks as if he wanted to pass stolen jewels off, and when you asked for assurances about his right to them he backed down."

"Yes," Mannering agreed stiffly.

"John," Lorna said. "John, did he always come alone?"

"Yes."

"Did he—did he talk about anyone else in with him?"

"No," Mannering said. "He said that he was staying at the Overseas Club, and twice I left messages for him there. He picked them up all right." Mannering's mind was beginning to work more swiftly and clearly, and there was a more confident note in his voice. "He tried me out and found that I wouldn't handle stolen stuff, and then— he died. I could understand it more if he were alive."

"Understand what more?" demanded Lloyd.

"The planting of the other jewels," Mannering said. "I could understand it if he were planning to blackmail me, but—it's far too late. Even if he were alive, it would be too late now that the police have made this charge."

He was rubbing his hand across his forehead, looking at Lorna, but trying not to think about her, and what the next week was going to mean to her. "Someone killed Blest," he went on. "Someone killed Farmer. How did Klein *alias* Laker die? Lorna—Lloyd! Listen to me. someone killed Blest and Farmer, and the same man might have killed Laker. So we want the murderer—it's the one defence I've got. Is Chittering with us?"

"He'll do anything he can."

"Get him to plug that line by implication—I'm not the murderer, so the murderer is still at large. As soon as Larraby can get about, have him go to his friends in the trade—we need to find friends of Klein *alias* Laker. Have the girl Blest and have the motor-cyclist Terry McKay closely watched and followed. If there's nearly half a million pounds worth of stolen jewellery hidden away, someone is going to release it on to the market."

He stopped speaking.

He saw from Lorna's expression, as well as from the solicitor's, that he had not moved them to hope. And he knew exactly why. He had told them to do the obvious things, only the obvious things, and much more was needed.

What did they expect him to do? Work a miracle?

Lorna said: "We'll do everything, darling, everything we can, but—working without you will be like working with one arm."

As she stopped, the door opened, and after a pause, Bristow said:

"Ready, Mannering?"

15

REMAND CELL

MANNERING said: "Yes, Bill, I'm ready." He put his hands out to Lorna again, and she rested hers in his, trying not to grip too hard, trying not to show too much emotion. If she showed too much, it would suggest that she felt frightened of what might follow, that she had no confidence in the outcome, "'Bye for now, darling," Mannering went on. "It won't be long. It's the worst one we've had to face, because we don't know what it's all about, but we'll find out." He kissed her, squeezed her hands again, and turned away. "All right," he said to Bristow, who opened the door wide. Two uniformed policemen were outside, and a man wearing a peaked cap—a warder from Brixton. Some wag further along the passage called out:

"All aboard for Brixton Jail!"

Mannering walked side by side with Bristow, the warder in front, the two policemen behind.

"John," Bristow said, "we only want to catch the guilty."

"Tell that to Ingleby."

"It's true, and you know it."

"Not this time," retorted Mannering. "Ingleby and the others have forgotten how to be objective. They've taken sides already."

"If you tell me of any clue which I can follow up to help you, I'll see that it's done."

"Not this time," Mannering said again. The warder reached the door leading to the street; it was ajar. He pushed it wide open, on to the bright sunlit buildings, on to the Black Maria pulled up outside, on to a crowd of hundreds of people, and cameramen jostling each other. A newsreel or television camera was placed on top of a

van on the right, another across the road. There was a
roaring kind of sound as Mannering appeared. "Now I
know what the gladiators felt like," Mannering said, and
raised his voice: "Bristow, I don't think I can rely on a
square deal."

"*Anything for us, Mannering?*" a newspaperman called.

"*Any idea who really did it, Mannering?*"

"*Hold it!*"

The police were outside in strength, pushing the crowd
back. Lights were flashing. The movie cameras were
whirring. Some teen-age girls were giving vent to the
squeals usually reserved for singing idols. Chittering was
on the fringe of the crowd. Even in this situation, he
managed to raise his hand in that reassuring thumb and
forefinger salute. "We'll get you out," he seemed to say.

A passage was cleared through the crowd to the Black
Maria. Newspapermen were rapping out questions to
Mannering, who raised his hand to them, and smiled,
actually laughed as one of the cameramen tripped over
the kerb. The doors of the big black van opened, and
Mannering saw two uniformed men inside; otherwise it
was empty.

"Specially reserved for me, is it?" he asked, and
climbed up into the van. The girls squealed again, a man
called:

"*Hang all murderers, that's what I say.*"

One of the men held Mannering's arm, the other
closed the doors. In here it was very dark after the
brightness of the street, and the sounds were cut off, too.
Mannering lowered himself to one of the bench seats,
leaned back with his head touching the van, and closed
his eyes.

The engine started up and the van began to move
slowly. He stayed there with his eyes closed. He could not
think, yet; the situation was too vividly emotional. What
must Lorna be feeling? He could still feel the pressure of
her fingers, see the strain in her eyes. How long ago was
it that he'd talked to her on the telephone without a

thought of anxiety? How long ago was it since she had come into the flat, speaking flippantly to Ingleby, because she had been so sure that nothing really serious could happen?

The van gathered speed.

"You all right, Mr. Mannering?" one of the warders asked.

The "Mister" did Mannering good, in a ridiculous way; it told of a kind of respect, told that this man did not regard him as one of the unending trail of prisoners who were conveyed from here to Brixton Jail. Mannering opened his eyes.

"Yes, thanks. I'm as well as can be expected."

"Fag?"

"Nice of you," said Mannering. He took a cigarette from a familiar packet, accepted a light, then stretched out his legs. "How long does it take to get there?"

"Half an hour or so," the warder replied. "It's all according to the traffic. It won't be so bad when you get there. On remand you can have what you want sent in, and they're easy with visitors, too. The present Governor's okay at the moment—the last one was a bit of a bastard."

Mannering remembered meeting "the last one" at several social functions, and the remark amused him. Now that the immediate crisis was past, he felt less tense, and gradually began to think more objectively—not of what to do, but of how to start finding out the best plan of campaign.

With Larraby out of action, and the other staff immature, Chittering would be the best man to help. The newspaperman would actually have a double motive to help, and also to get a scoop for the *Daily Globe*. Lorna, Chittering, Tom as legman, and Lloyd as liaison between them and Brixton Jail. The cold fact that he would be unable to do anything for himself suddenly became more vivid, and his brief mood of relaxation passed.

How could he rely on the others to work at second hand? How could he hope to direct their activities if he could make no inquiries himself? He did not even know where to start.

If he were to have a chance, he must get out of Brixton.

Supposing he managed to escape? It would be difficult, but not impossible; few men knew more about the ways and means of escaping, of picking locks, of forcing windows. What would follow?

If he escaped and could establish his innocence—nothing important. If he failed, then he would be for ever on the run. Lorna would never know what it was like to have a feeling of security and safety. Sooner or later he would be caught, too; the continual feeling of being hunted might even make him give himself up.

So, should he try to escape?

If he did, and if he failed to clear himself, the world would judge him guilty. Up to the moment when he had appeared in court, escape would have had its advantages, but now—would it bring anything but risks and added dangers?

The charge was *murder*, remember.

The warder opposite him broke a long silence.

"Nearly there," he declared. "Next stop will be the gates."

Mannering wrenched his thoughts off the future, to cope with the immediate present. He could not see the great doors of the prison, but knew them well enough. The Black Maria stopped. Men spoke, then there was the sound of opening gates, the unmistakable rattle of keys, the hard voice of authority, then a squeaking sound. The van moved forward slowly, then stopped again. Mannering felt his tension rise to screaming point. One of the warders unlocked the door and threw them open on to a bare bleak yard, with high walls and those massive gates.

Two more warders came up to take charge of him.

. . . . .

"Mr. Mannering," the Governor said. "Certain regulations have to be observed, but within them we like to make things as easy as we can for anyone on remand. You can send out for special food, cigarettes, for anything you like within reason and of course you will wear your own clothes . . ."

The warder had known his man.

Mannering stepped into his cell. There was a narrow bed, an upright and an armchair, a small table, every "comfort". And there was the atmosphere of prison, a curiously antiseptic kind of odour, a hushed silence which all noises broke harshly. The door was of iron, and there was a grille, above head height, but no window.

On remand or not, this was prison. He felt as if the walls were closing in on him, as if the ceiling was creeping lower and lower. When the door was locked and the warder went away, he felt an overpowering sense of loneliness and of restriction. For that first hour it seemed as if the bottom had dropped out of his world. His mind fogged up, he felt almost panic-striken—and all he wanted was to get out.

It *must* be possible.

The risks and the dangers did not matter. Any risk was better than staying here, helpless, damned. How could he expect anyone outside to find the vital evidence he needed? How could anyone else do what he had to do himself?

"I've got to get away," he whispered. "I can't take it— I've got to get away."

.   .   .   .

"I know Mannering very well," Bristow said to the Governor of the Prison. "He is an accomplished escapologist, a specialist in forcing locks, and a man of great physical courage as well as surprising ingenuity. Sooner or later, I think he'll try to escape."

"I'll see that he doesn't succeed," the Governor said grimly. "I'll have him watched very closely indeed."

.   .   .   .

Lorna opened the door of the Green Street flat, and Ethel came hurrying from the kitchen, her hands wet, her face flushed. She took one look at Chittering behind Lorna, and said huskily:

"So they kept him, ma'am."

"Yes, Ethel," Lorna replied. "For a little while."

"I was praying he'd come back with you," Ethel said. Lorna could see that she was close to tears, and hoped desperately that she wouldn't break down; her own sense of frustration, of failure, of fear, was so acute. "I really was, ma'am, and—"

"Any messages, Ethel?" interrupted Chittering, sensing Lorna's mood.

"Only some newspapermen, and—oh, yes, there's a call coming through from New York, from a Mr. Pleydell. He's supposed to ring again at one o'clock. That's everything, ma'am."

Lorna thought: Toby's heard, then. She went into John's study, looked round drearily, and heard Chittering just behind her. "Chitty," she said. "What are we going to do?"

"We're going to get John out," Chittering declared. "Lorna, there's one thing of vital importance in this case. Absolutely vital importance."

"Well?"

"He mustn't escape," Chittering said. "I've talked to Bristow, who expects him to try. I've talked to my Editor, who'll be pro-John provided John doesn't make a break. But in a desperate situation like this he might think it's his only chance. He mustn't."

"Could we ever stop him?" Lorna demanded.

"This time I think we must," Chittering said.

.   .   .   .

The line from New York was as clear as if from a house round the corner, and Toby Pleydell's deep voice was firm and definite.

"You sit tight, Lorna, and I'll be back by this time tomorrow. Yes, I've booked my plane. Now listen, there's one thing of vital importance. I know John almost as well as you do, and the likely thing for him to try is to escape, so as to get busy himself. Tell him he mustn't. Make him realise it would be a fatal mistake."

Lorna didn't speak.

"Are you there?" Toby demanded.

"Yes," Lorna said, hesitantly. "Yes, Toby—why?"

"Why what?"

"Why does everyone want to keep John in prison?"

"It's for his own good."

"But *why*?"

Pleydell said, almost desperately: "If you can't see for yourself, I don't see how I can make you. John has taken chances before and got away with them, but there's been nothing like this. I spent an hour on the telephone with Lloyd this morning, so I know the situation as well as Lloyd does. If the bulk of the jewels are found, giving a lead to the real guilty party, we have a very good defence. If they're not found it will be tougher. There must be someone who saw the man Farmer come to the house. He must have been brought in a car by at least one other person. Once we can find a single witness to say that a car arrived at the crucial time, we'll have created an element of doubt, and the right counsel will have a good chance of getting an acquittal. But if John escapes, he'll be doing himself inestimable harm with the jury."

"But the jury isn't even thought of yet!"

"The jury is alive and kicking, and reading the newspapers," Pleydell said grimly. "If John escapes and doesn't find the evidence he wants, he won't stand a chance of acquittal. He must be made to understand that."

From the extension in the hall, Chittering called:

"He's right, Lorna."

"Who's there with you?" demanded Pleydell sharply.

"Chitty."

"Talk it over with him," Pleydell urged. "And whatever you do, get word to John that he mustn't escape—at least until I've talked to him."

Lorna said heavily: "All right, Toby."

"That's my girl!" There was a pause. "I know it's no use saying take it easy, but—take it easy, my dear. Good-bye."

"Good-bye," Lorna said slowly. She put the receiver down, and stared out of the window at the houses across the street, until Chittering came and joined her. After a long silence, she went on: "It's like a conspiracy of all his friends and enemies combined—first to get him into prison, then to keep him there."

"Now listen," Chittering said, protestingly. "*You* know it would be crazy for him to escape. You would normally be the first one to say so."

"Would I?" Lorna asked, and went on heavily: "I suppose you're right. And I suppose the truth is that I can't see anybody but John himself getting out of this mess. Unless Josh Larraby—"

She broke off.

"I'll try to find out if there's any news of Josh," Chittering promised. "I'll call you soon."

When he had gone, Lorna spent ten minutes in her bedroom, before going to join Ethel in the kitchen. Ethel's face seemed to grow longer all the time, and she kept sniffing. Lorna went over and over everything she knew, trying to see the situation as John would.

Lloyd telephoned. He was going to see John this afternoon; had she any special message? "*Don't escape, don't escape,*" seemed a refrain in Lorna's mind, and it was some time before she answered. "Just tell him Toby will be here tomorrow," she said.

"Right, Mrs. Mannering. And I'll try to arrange for you to see him soon."

"Thank you," Lorna said, formally.

She rang off again, and saw that it was half-past two. She felt heavy-eyed and physically tired; undoubtedly she would be wise to try to rest. She slipped off her dress and loosened her girdle, then lay down on the bed, sure that she wouldn't doze off; but she did, and woke with a start, to see Ethel bending over her anxiously.

"I'm sorry to wake you, but it's Mr. Chittering," Ethel said. "And he says it's very urgent."

"Chitty?" Lorna sat up in bed, glanced at herself in the dressing-table mirror, slipped out of bed, ran a comb through her hair, pulled on a dressing-gown, and went out. Chittering was in the study, and the moment she saw him, hope died. She had never seen him looking so glum.

"What is it?" she demanded, and steeled herself to take whatever blow was coming now.

"I hardly know how to tell you," Chittering said, and his voice had a hoarse, nervous note. "The truth is—er, the truth is, Josh has come round."

"But that's just what we want!"

"It's what we thought we wanted," Chittering replied, and cold fear gripped Lorna. "But he says he can't remember anything at all—that his mind's a complete blank from the time he left Covent Garden last night. The police believe he's clamming up to avoid saying what he knows."

16

LORNA PLEADS

"Josh," Lorna pleaded, "try to remember."

The old man lay in bed at a nursing home not far from the flat in Chelsea, where he had been transferred by the police. A policeman in plainclothes, with a pencil in his hand and a notebook on his knees, sat in a corner of the room. Lorna sat on one side of Larraby's bed, a hand resting on his thin, white arm. He looked very pale, a ghost of himself. His eyes held a vacant look; Lorna felt quite sure that he was not pretending. He really could not remember. That drove her even closer to utter desperation.

"Josh—"

"I'm sorry, Mrs. Mannering," Larraby said; his voice was very weak. "If I could remember, I would tell you, but I don't. I simply don't. I went to the opera last night, I do remember that—if it *was* last night." He pressed his hand against his forehead and closed his eyes; when he opened them again, they seemed filled with pain, and their expression was vague and haunted. "I don't remember when it was, I just remember that it was the day that Rebecca Blest came to see Mr. Mannering, he was so troubled because she had brought him false jewels."

The policeman began to write.

"Josh," Lorna said, and she tried to keep the note of urgency out of her voice, for fear of worrying Larraby too much, "did Mr. Mannering show you those jewels?"

Josh stared.

"Did he, Josh?"

"No," replied Larraby, and his voice fell away to a whisper. "He came out of the office and told me what had happened. I could have seen the jewels if I'd wished, of course, but there was no need. Mr. Mannering would know whether the jewels were genuine or not, far better than I. Why do you ask?"

Lorna said: "I'm very anxious to know."

"Is Mr. Mannering in trouble?"

"In a kind of trouble—" Lorna began, and the policeman in the corner coughed warningly; she had been allowed here to question Larraby provided only that she did not tell him what had happened. "But he's been in trouble before, Josh."

"How well I know it," Larraby said. "I wish I could be up and about, to help him, but I feel so—so weak, so terribly weak. I've never been like this before, Mrs. Mannering. Will—will you answer me a simple question truthfully?"

There were so many that Lorna wanted to ask, but she said:

"If I can, Josh."

He moved his hand to take hers, hitched himself up a little on his pillows, and asked: "Have I had a stroke, Mrs. Mannering? That's what I rather suspect. Am I dangerously ill?"

"The doctors say you haven't had a stroke, and you'll be perfectly all right if you rest," Lorna answered. "You mustn't worry about the shop, we'll manage there. Do you feel up to answering a few more questions?"

"I think so, Mrs. Mannering."

"Did you see the man Klein when he came into Quinns?"

"Well, yes, I did once," answered Larraby. "I had a strange feeling that I had seen him before somewhere, but I couldn't recollect where, one's memory isn't so reliable at my age. I did mention it to Mr. Mannering in passing, but it was of no significance. Usually I was out when Mr. Klein called. I understood that he was hoping that Mr. Mannering would act for him in some substantial private sales, but nothing came of it."

"Do you know why it didn't?"

"No," replied Larraby, after a pause. "No, except that

Mr. Mannering said that he thought the man was trying to get service on the cheap."

"I see. And last night—you really don't remember anything?"

Larraby hitched himself further up on his elbows, looked at Lorna very straightly, and asked:

"What am I supposed to remember, Mrs. Mannering? What has happened? Why are you here instead of Mr. Mannering himself?"

Lorna said: "They weren't false jewels, they were real ones—and stolen. That's what the police say, anyhow. They were found—"

"I'd rather you didn't make that statement," said the man who was taking notes. "That's giving a lead."

Larraby turned on him testily: "What does it matter if she gives me a lead? What has happened?"

Lorna said: "Josh, Mr. Mannering is in Brixton Jail, on remand on a serious charge. You may be able to help him if you can only remember what happened after you got home last night—and after you left Covent Garden. Try to remember."

"I'll remember, somehow," Larraby said, vehemently. But he dropped back on his pillows as if the news had shocked him badly. He could not stop himself from closing his eyes.

.   .   .   .

"So old Josh doesn't remember," Mannering said, in a hard voice. "And you really think it's genuine loss of memory?"

"I'm sure it is," Lorna told him. "I can't believe he's pretending."

"It could be induced. The amatyl drug can do that. Not that it helps us." Mannering paused. "Everything's coming at once, isn't it?" He looked at Lloyd, who had already told him that Pleydell was on his way, and glanced at the warder who was at the door, able to hear everything that was said. It was a precious enough privilege to see Lorna; he knew that he must take no risk of offending the Governor's ruling—that all conversation with her must be clearly audible. He saw that Lorna looked rested, her eyes a little less bright; but her tension was alarming in itself. He said almost inanely: "We'll have to put our thinking caps on, won't we?"

"John," Lorna said.

"Yes, my sweet?"

"Do you remember—what happened in 1949?"

"1949?" echoed Mannering, and frowned. "No, I can't say that offhand—" He broke off, recollection flooding sudden and swift—recollection that in 1949 he had been on the point of arrest, inside Scotland Yard, with Bristow about to charge him. He had fooled Bristow, climbed out of the office and escaped from the Yard. Later that night, he had found the proof he wanted of his innocence. He felt a new tension, because it seemed as if Lorna was telling him that he would have to do that again. "Oh, yes," he added, and forced a laugh which sounded natural. "I remember. Why?"

"You mustn't—" Lorna began, and glanced at the warder then at Lloyd, bit her underlip, and went on: "It wouldn't be so easy or so safe, John. You've got to think of something new. That's vital."

"Something new," Mannering echoed. "Something new?" He realised at once what she meant, knew exactly what Lloyd had been hinting at earlier. They would know what his reaction was likely to be, would know that above everything else—he wanted to get out of here, to hunt for the killer and for those jewels.

"John—"

"All right, my sweet," Mannering said. "I'm very anxious to see Toby, anyhow—no offence, Lloyd. When do you say he's due?"

"He'll be here in the morning."

"Everyone's rallied round, anyhow," Mannering said. "How are the newspapers?"

"They've got it all over the front pages, but they haven't taken sides yet," Lloyd said. "Mrs. Mannering, I think we should go—we mustn't overstay our welcome."

Mannering gave a brittle kind of laugh.

"Welcome! No, that would never do. Tactfully said, Lloyd. Sorry. All right, my sweet. I have a little sense left, and I'll remember 1949."

When they had gone, he sat down on the upright chair and looked at the iron door with its iron grille, and which kept him out of the passage. He could still hear their footsteps, but that was unimportant compared with the significance of what Lorna had urged. "Don't escape," she had pleaded, and there wasn't much doubt that she had been put up to that. "*Don't escape, don't escape.*" At least they acknowledged the probability that he could. Of course he could! He had been here a whole day, now; he had studied all the movements of the warders; he had examined that lock on the door. With patience he could get a strand or two of wire off a window grille, and could unlock this door in a few seconds, without much trouble. He felt sure that if he chose the moment rightly he could walk out of here. In the event, it probably wouldn't be so easy as he told himself, but if he had once broken out of Scotland Yard, he could from here.

"*Don't escape,*" Lorna had said. "*Don't escape.*"

Find some other way of saving his neck!

Lloyd had said plenty, too, before Lorna had come in. "As things are at the moment, Mr. Mannering, I am quite sure that we have a very good chance of establishing your innocence. We don't know what new circumstances might turn up, of course."

Such as an attempt at escape.

Lloyd had talked Lorna into that advice, he had convinced her that it was wise.

Everything in Mannering called out to pick this lock, and to get out of here. If necessary he must overpower the guard and take the keys of other doors, but—supposing he succeeded? What would happen? Had Lloyd virtually been telling him that he would be throwing away the chance that he had now? Was that the reason for his insistence that the talk with Toby Pleydell, tomorrow, was of extreme importance?

Mannering felt sweat beading his forehead. The warder was peering at him through the grille, as if perturbed by what he saw. He made himself light a cigarette, drew in deeply, exhaled slowly.

If he couldn't get out of here, what *could* he do?

He made himself answer.

He could decide what had to be done, and find a way of making the others do it. He could come to grips with the problem here as well as anywhere else. It was easy to be swept off his feet by emotional anxiety, by the shock of what had happened, but somewhere behind all this must be a rational explanation, waiting to be discovered.

"Make your mind work," he abjured himself savagely. "Make it *work*."

.   .   .   .

"What's the man Mannering been like?" asked a senior warder, when the daytime warder went off duty. "Any change in him since his wife and solicitor came to see him?"

"In a way there is," the other man answered. "He kept muttering to himself for a while, and paced up and down a bit. Then he sat down and began to write, screwed up the paper, and started all over again. He's been at it for an hour or more. If you ask me, he's got the wind up."

"Any sign that he might try to escape?"

"Not a thing," the warder assured him. "I know all the tricks they get up to, and he hasn't used one yet."

.   .   .   .

Mannering put a dish of ice-cream, half finished, on to the dinner tray, then pushed his chair back from the table, stood up, and lit a cigarette, with the same harsh drawing of smoke that betrayed his tension. Yet he felt calmer. The result of his thinking was down in black and white, and he could hand the notes to Toby Pleydell and Lloyd in the morning. There wasn't really a great deal, nothing startlingly new, but at least he had been able to marshall the facts clearly, and to write down what needed doing.

He picked up a writing pad, and read:

1. Trace the man or men who brought Farmer to (a) the house or (b) to the flat. *Job for Chittering.*
2. Trace a neighbour or passer-by who saw a car arrive at about 8 o'clock last evening. Alternatively, find neighbours who heard a car in the street. *Job for Tom, supported by Chitty.*
3. Check Rebecca Blest, her father, and all other relatives. *Job for Lloyd/Pleydell/an Inquiry Agency.*
4. Check all associates of Rett Laker, before and after his imprisonment, get names of his prison associates, anyone with whom he might have made plans about finding or disposing of the jewels when released from prison. *Job for Inquiry Agency. Police might help.*

Mannering looked up from the list and closed his eyes against a new rush of fear. The savage truth was that even if there were a development from Point 4, someone outside would have to follow it up. He did not know anyone but himself who could; no one else would take such desperate chances. Why should they? No one else had his specialised ability, either, except, to a degree, the police.

He read on:

5. Check Larraby's movements last night and find out if he was away from his apartment. Check for his fingerprints on the two books which were disturbed—Collis's *Regency Jewellery* and *Handbook of American Jewel Merchants. Possible job for Chitty.*

6. Check everything possible about the youth Terence McKay. Check nature of the meeting. Find the constable whom the girl said spoke to them, ask the Yard to find out from him if the encounter between McKay and R.B. had seemed accidental—as Tom has said.

7. Find out why I've been framed—what good will it do anyone?!

He put the pad down and picked up his pen, adding:

8. Was Farmer the man who telephoned me saying he could give me the genuine jewellery? If so, why was he killed?

9. Find out how man got into Blest's flat in Notting Hill. Find out what means of forcing entry was used. Find out if any other jewellery found at the flat as a result of the police search. *Job for Chittering.*

10. Find out if Rebecca Blest could have been putting on an act. Find out if she had any associates among criminals, her boy friends, the lot. *Job (a) for Lorna (b) for Inquiry Agency.*

Although he did not write it down, there was a job for him; if anything was found against the girl or young McKay, who could follow the information up? Who could work on it until the full significance was known? *He* could.

If he were free.

He made himself write on:

11. Find out if Klein *alias* Laker called in person at the Overseas Club for those messages. If not, who did? And why use the Overseas Club?

12. What has caused Larraby's loss of memory? (if it is genuine). Shock—injury—drug? Get a medical opinion.

13. Why did Klein *alias* Laker really come to Quinns? Did he want to do a deal through me? Was there deeper significance in the man's visits than there appeared?

17

ONE BY ONE

"No, I'm sorry, Mrs. Mannering," said the little woman with the mop of grey hair. "I didn't hear anything that night. But then, I had the television on, and you don't hear anything outside with that on, do you? I do wish I could help you. I'm sure it must be very worrying to have Mr. Mannering in this plight."

Lorna said mechanically: "Yes, it is. Thank you, Mrs. Grey."

"Oh, that's a pleasure. As a matter of fact, Mrs. Cornhill, next door but one, asked me the same question only this morning. I believe a newspaperman had been worrying her about it. Everyone in the street is very anxious to help. We all feel so proud of Mr. Mannering."

"You're very good," said Lorna. She forced a smile, and turned away. "Good night." It was after six o'clock. She was tired, her mouth was dry, her feet ached because she had been walking to and fro, or standing and talking to people in Green Street, for the past three hours. This was her own particular assignment, and it seemed to be as futile as the rest. No one could remember hearing a car, or seeing anyone walk from a car to the house, or walk along the street. Green Street seemed to have been peopled by ghosts about the time that the man Farmer had come to the flat.

There was one more house, with two flats in it. She called at the ground floor one. An elderly man whom she knew by sight kept her on the doorstep, said that he had already told the police that he had noticed nothing unusual on the evening in question, and good night. The door closed sharply, nearly slammed. Lorna hesitated, then went up the stairs towards the first floor flat. She had been received pleasantly by most of the neighbours, but a few had been like this man: not openly hostile, simply aloof. They thought John guilty, of course.

As she approached the higher flat, she heard a child crying. A squealing infant was the last thing she wanted to cope with now. Another child called out, shrilly. Lorna hesitated, with a finger at the door, and as she did so she heard the street door open again, and a man come hurrying up. She recognised a plump, merry-faced, youngish man, who left the house on the tick of eight o'clock every morning. He stopped short.

"Can I help—oh, Mrs. Mannering!"

"I wanted to ask your wife a question or two, but she seems to have her hands full," Lorna said.

"Oh, Meg's used to that," the man declared. "Noisy brats, aren't they?" He thrust his key into the door, pushed the door open, and raised his voice to a stentorian: *"Daddy's home!"*

The shrill calling, and even the baby's crying, ceased. A long-legged girl of seven or eight, and a plump boy of four or five, came flying out of a room on the right, as if intent on bringing their father down. By some trick, he managed to hoist each of them shoulder-high, the girl in his right arm, the boy on his left. At the same moment, a very tiny woman, who looked too young to be married, came hurrying out of the room, with a baby in her arms— the baby naked except for a napkin. She stopped short at sight of Lorna.

"Why, Bert! Why didn't you tell me?"

"We met on the doorstep," her husband explained. "Okay, kids, that's enough. Popsie, take Simple Simon from your mother for five minutes—any objection to the *enfants terribles* hearing, Mrs. Mannering?"

Lorna said faintly: "None at all."

"Always better to let 'em listen. It's guaranteed to keep 'em quiet for at least ten minutes," Bert said. His mastery over his children was remarkable to see. He found time to tickle the naked baby on its plump little belly before leading the way into a room on the right.

It was a living-room, with piles of toys in one corner, everything out of place, the mantelpiece crowded with letters, ornaments, bills, matches, two bottles, and some birthday cards obviously for one of the children, on which the numeral 5 was displayed.

"Sit down, Mrs. Mannering," Bert invited, and pushed a chair into position; the child-like mother cleared another chair and sat down. "The police were here last night, and a newspaperman this morning—wasn't he, Meg?"

"A Mr. Chittering," Meg remembered. She had huge eyes, very dark blue.

"I know they've been worrying you," said Lorna, "but I feel I must try to do something myself. I expect you know that a great deal will turn on whether this man Farmer was attacked before he reached Green Street—or, rather, before he went upstairs to our apartment."

"That's what the police hinted," said Bert. "They're fair enough, Mrs. Mannering. They tried to find out, all right, but there wasn't a thing we could tell them. I don't mind admitting that by the time we get the mob to bed, we're just about exhausted. This room is at the back of the house, too—we collapse and listen to television until bed time. The night before last was our usual routine."

"I only wish we could help," the little woman said, as if she meant it.

"I'm sure you do," said Lorna, and did her best not to speak mechanically. "It's a dead hour between nine and ten o'clock. I suppose that's why no one noticed anything."

There may have been nothing noticeable to remember, she reminded herself glumly. But if two had been "helping" a third to the doorway, for instance—

"Funny thing about not noticing," remarked Bert, briskly. "I was reading a life of a Scotland Yard chap the other day—dare say your husband knew him, Mrs. Mannering, chap named Bell—and he was saying how many people miss what goes on under their noses, but remember it if something happens to jog their memory properly. I'll tell you what—I'll go and have a chat with some of the neighbours tonight, get them talking. It's amazing what comes out when half a dozen people start a get-together. We know the Lampleys and the Cornhills and the Robbs. They all live nearly opposite your place. Something might make them remember if they saw or heard a car."

Lorna said: "You're very good."

"Think nothing of it," said Bert, cheerfully. "Only too glad to help Mr. Mannering if we can—we're very proud of him in Green Street, you know."

"Proud?" echoed Lorna.

"Kind of reflected glory, you could say," explained Bert, crisply. "Can I get you a cup of tea?"

"I must be going," Lorna said. "Thank you very much indeed, Mr.—" She realised suddenly that she didn't know his surname, yet they had been neighbours for years!

She saw him grin.

"Entwhistle," he informed her. "Good old north country name, Mrs. Mannering."

Lorna crossed Green Street a few minutes later, glancing up at the houses on the other side of the street. A few years ago there had been an empty site here, and her house with two others had been the only ones left standing after a bombing raid. Now, a block of flats was being built, and they would have to move before long, so that these houses could be demolished to make room for another block; she and John had two more years on their lease. The new flats weren't yet finished, and the builders had left huge piles of sand and gravel, great stacks of bricks and timber, on the site, which showed up eerily in the lamplight.

Lorna went upstairs, thinking how little she knew of the neighbours. Everyone in Green Street could have been forgiven for thinking she and John were hopeless snobs. Well, weren't they? *"We're very proud of him in Green Street, you know."*

A car turned the corner, as Lorna waited on the porch. It slowed down and stopped opposite her, and Chittering called:

"That you, Lorna?"

"Hallo, Chitty."

"Had any luck?" Chittering closed the car door and came towards her with his long stride.

"Nothing at all," Lorna answered. "Absolutely nothing at all."

"Ruddy people never keep their eyes open," Chittering complained. He took her key from her, opened the street door, and gave the key back. The lift was on the ground floor. There was only just room for the two of them, and it crawled up to their floor. Chittering pushed open the gate. "Never feel I dare talk in that lift," he remarked. "I always think that if I breathe too heavily it might stop." He saw the front door of the flat open, and Ethel appeared.

"Here we are, Ethel," Lorna said.

"Have you had any good news, ma'am?" Ethel inquired eagerly.

"Not yet, I'm afraid."

"Well, it's only the matter of time, I'm convinced of that," said Ethel, with determined optimism. "I must say it's been as trying as it possibly can, now that Mr. Pleydell's been delayed."

"*What?*"

"That's one of the things I had to tell you," said Chittering, unhappily. "There's heavy fog at New York, and both the airports are out of action. Toby will be twenty-four hours late at least."

Lorna didn't feel that she could speak.

"Will you stay to dinner, Mr. Chittering?" asked Ethel, anxious to change the subject.

"If I'm not being a nuisance."

"You must stay, Chitty," Lorna made herself say. She took off her hat with a weary gesture which had almost become characteristic, and went towards her bedroom. "Help yourself to a drink. I won't be five minutes." From the door, she asked: "Did Mr. Lloyd say he was coming round tonight, Ethel?"

"Yes, ma'am, about nine o'clock."

After he had been to Brixton, Lorna thought miserably. She dropped on to the dressing-table stool, kicked off her shoes, wriggled her toes, and for a few moments felt as if all she wanted to do was to stretch out on the bed and try to sleep. Eventually she got up, washed, put on powder and a dab of rouge and lipstick, changed her shoes, and hurried back to the study, where Chittering was nursing a whisky-and-soda.

"Pour me a sherry, will you?" Lorna asked, and stretched out her hands to the coal fire. She watched Chitty pour, took the drink, and went on: "I suppose it's all bad news, or you would have told me by now."

"It's one dead end after another," growled Chittering. "Enough to drive you to drink." He forced a laugh. "Want it straight?"

"Please."

"Right. Tom and I have been working, Lloyd's private inquiry contact has been busy, too, and the *Globe's* detailed a couple of chaps to help. And it's still blank, blank, blank. Take Rebecca Blest and her father. She seems completely genuine. She's a typist in an office, and earns ten pounds seven a week. Her father worked for forty-three years in the same shipping company, as a clerk, and retired on a small pension. They had no money to speak of until this legacy. They inherited all of Rett Laker's estate, and at first thought it was worth next to nothing. The jewellery seems to have been a complete surprise to them. There isn't much doubt that there's something phoney about the legacy. No jewels were *mentioned* in the will, and we don't know that the girl's father told her all he knew. Probably he knew the truth, and knew that nearly half a million pounds worth is stashed away somewhere. Not that it helps us much now."

Lorna said: "No, I suppose not."

"Then, this Terence McKay. I've seen him, Tom's seen

him, and Lloyd's agent has, too. He works in an engineer-
ing supplies warehouse. He was out on errand on Tuesday
afternoon, with permission to go home when he'd finished
his last delivery. There isn't the slightest indication that
he'd ever seen Rebecca Blest until Tuesday afternoon.
None of the neighbours has noticed him—not even the
Ashtons who live downstairs, the family with the lanky
daughter and her whining voice."

"I know the one you mean," said Lorna.

"I'll bet you do! Her father has appointed himself a
kind of Protector of Rebecca—she's going to move downstairs with them until everything's over. Neighbours can
be decent, and even the clots have kind hearts." Chittering
pursed his lips. "Next, Josh Larraby. He might have
taken some amytal, a drug which causes short term
amnesia—loss of memory for a short period—and can
cause it spasmodically. There's no way of being sure,
now. It would be out of his bloodstream before the
doctors suspected what caused his trouble. If he'd had
blood tests and all the rest yesterday morning the medics
might have been able to tell, but not now. There's no
certainty about anything except that he genuinely doesn't
remember."

Lorna closed her eyes.

Ethel said timidly, from the door: "Dinner's all ready,
Mrs. Mannering."

She had cooked a chicken to perfection. Lorna picked
at it, and noticed wryly that the situation didn't stop
Chittering from eating heartily; now and again he
slowed down, as if almost ashamed to demonstrate that
he was so hale, hearty and unaffected.

He kept up a running commentary.

". . . can't be sure of the fingerprints on those two
books which John told us about. They're being checked
with Larraby's, now—the police raised no objection to us
taking the books as they'd already finished. They aren't
exactly being co-operative, but they aren't being really
obstructive."

"I should think not!"

"Tell you one thing that Bristow did let out," said Larraby. "In Farmer's pockets there was a note of this telephone number, and they've found a C.I.D. man who noticed Farmer near a call box at Hyde Park—they're thorough, you see. It was almost certainly Farmer who telephoned John and said he had the real jewels. Not that Bristow admits that he called about the real jewels, but he admits that Farmer might well have been the man who telephoned here. I saw Bristow myself, and tried to find out if there's anything new known about Laker *alias* Klein's associates since Laker came out of prison. Apparently he lived in a small flat in Fulham. He saw his brother-in-law a few times, but practically no one else. He's not been in touch with any of his pre-prison-day friends at all—in fact as Klein he kept to himself, except for these regular visits to Quinns and to his brother-in-law, Blest."

After a pause, Lorna asked: "Does John know all of this?"

"Lloyd's been told everything, and should be telling John about now."

"So we've really drawn an absolute blank," Lorna said. It was hard to get the words out.

" 'Fraid so," agreed Chittering, unhappily. "The one thing that could lead to something is from the Overseas Club. The messages for Klein weren't collected by Laker *alias* Klein himself—they were collected by a coloured youth, who is a member of the club. He hasn't been in for nearly a month—not since Laker died—and the club's promised to let me know if he turns up again. I expect the police have made the same request, too. Oh—one other thing. Bristow's puzzled because a picture Larraby used to have on the wall of his hall, just behind the front door, has disappeared. It's a peculiar thing—the nail for it was hanging on the wall, but the picture's vanished. It's possible that he took it away himself, of course, but— well, there was some broken glass in the passage, too. Did you notice any?"

"I thought there was some on the floor," Lorna said. "How did you find that out?"

"Bristow wanted to know if I'd seen any picture there. Larraby's cleaning woman told him, eventually—I don't know whether Josh himself has been told about it." Chittering pushed his chair back, and looked moodily into Lorna's eyes. "I know how grim you must feel about all this. I couldn't be sorrier."

Lorna asked: "How do you think John feels?"

18

MANNERING PROPOSES

"AND that's everything," Mannering said to Geoffrey Lloyd.

"I'm afraid so, John."

"And Toby won't make it for at least another twenty-four hours," remarked Mannering, quite mildly. "Last night that would have made me want to hit the roof, Brixton must have a soothing effect." His smile was taut, in spite of what he said. "Well, let's see what we've got in the bag. This coloured chap who picked up the messages at the Overseas Club—will you see that your inquiry people and Chitty keep at that?"

"Of course."

"And the fact that Laker left his unspecified everything to his brother-in-law," said Mannering, intently. "Was Samuel Blest quite the innocent that we're told? Or did he know much more than he told his daughter? Why should Laker leave to a guileless brother-in-law an estate which might prove to be worth a fortune, unless he was sure that he could make the brother-in-law do whatever he wanted?" Mannering gave a brief smile. "Count that out, but the key question remains. Why did Laker leave the estate, including jewels which were not specified to—?"

He broke off, and his eyes brightened.

"Got something?" asked Lloyd.

"Could be an answer," Mannering said, softly. "If Samuel Blest was all his daughter thinks he was, then he would be the last man to be suspected of having these jewels. If Laker *alias* Klein had an accomplice, and there's no doubt he had, then they might have been anxious to have the estate in the hands of someone who

could easily be handled. So—" he broke off. "Leave that
one, for now. This broken glass at Josh Larraby's."

"Yes?"

"There was a picture behind that door all right. It was
a water-colour by Wimperis, a nice little meadow scene
which a client gave to Josh for buying for him at a sale. It
was in a black frame with a white border, and glazed.
Hasn't it turned up?"

"No. But the glass fragments have been examined—
it's ordinary window glass which is often used for glazing
pictures."

"I could understand it being broken, but not why it
should have been taken away," mused Mannering. "It
would be worth thirty or forty pounds, at the most, and
even then the buyer would have to want it keenly. So
we've got a missing coloured man and a missing water-
colour, and the puzzle of the inheritance. This man
Farmer, whom they think I killed—you say Bristow admits
that he had a note of my telephone number, and that he
may have used a phone box at Hyde Park Corner?"

"Yes."

"Any friends, associates, that kind of angle?"

"The police say he isn't known to them, and no one's
turned up to identify him, except a landlady who owns
the house in Whitechapel where he had a couple of rooms.
She says he kept himself to himself, and thinks he made
his money by betting. Our people can't find anything
much about him."

"No apparent association with Laker?"

"No."

"Any with a coloured man?"

"I don't know," said Lloyd. "It's a possibility—I'll
check."

"Thanks. And no news of anyone who saw a car in
Green Street?"

"No," answered Lloyd, unhappily. "Nothing at all.
The police have combed Green Street itself, so has
Chittering, and this evening I'm told that Lorna has been

visiting all the neighbours. But it isn't very likely that she would find out anything which the others have missed."

"I suppose not," said Mannering. "Except for one thing."

"What's that?"

"She'd give her right hand to find that witness," said Mannering. "Will you be seeing her tonight?"

"Yes."

"Geoffrey," Mannering said.

"Yes."

"Put an idea into her head, will you?"

"Yes."

"We need that witness more than we need anything else," Mannering went on, very softly, "and we need something to make anyone who did see anything, recall it. Also, the murderer must have accomplices, and crooks are notoriously greedy. Tell Lorna that it might be a good idea to offer a reward for anyone able to give information about what happened in Green Street on Tuesday night. A large reward. Let's say, ten thousand pounds."

Lloyd caught his breath.

"Not enough?" inquired Mannering.

"John," Lloyd said, with great deliberation, "if you offer a reward like that, and someone comes forward with the information, the police and the Public Prosecutor will say that you bribed the witness into making the statement. Prosecuting counsel will want to know why the witness didn't come forward until this large reward was offered." When Mannering didn't respond at once, he went on: "You can see that, surely?"

Mannering said: "Yes, I can see it. You know what you're doing, don't you?"

"What?"

"You're playing the police game."

"Now, John—"

"But you are," insisted Mannering. "Whether you know it or not, you're playing right into their hands. Don't escape, you say—don't try to do anything yourself, don't offer a sensational reward, don't do anything which might possibly give the prosecution a weaker hand if it comes to trial. Isn't that true?"

"Yes."

"Geoff," said Mannering, "you're making a big mistake."

"What mistake?"

"I didn't kill Farmer."

"I've never suggested—"

"You're working on the assumption that a trial is inevitable, because no evidence can be turned up to make it unnecessary. Nine times out of ten, ninety-nine times out of a hundred, you could be right—but this time you're wrong. I don't want to spend the next six or eight weeks in a remand cell waiting for trial. In six or eight weeks, before the Assizes could hear the case, Quinns would be virtually destroyed. Dealers all over the world would stop ordering from me. I'd lose nearly everything I possess, and most of what I've got is sunk in Quinns. Even if I were acquitted, the time lag between this moment and the acquittal would do the business serious damage. This isn't a job that we can sit on, and we don't have to worry about what prosecuting counsel might say to a jury. Everything we do must help to make sure that when I come up next Wednesday there is no case to answer."

"But it's a gambler's throw!"

"That's right," Mannering agreed. "I was always a gambler. Tell Lorna to put that reward out. Take a column in all the national newspapers, to advertise it. Say precisely what we need: evidence of anyone who saw a car stop outside any place in Green Street on Tuesday night between eight-thirty and nine-thirty in the evening. And make that reward very big, because it might bring a squeak from someone who's working for the murderer but won't get much of a cut in the profits."

Lloyd didn't respond, but backed slowly away from Mannering. He thrust one hand in his trousers pocket, frowned, and stared into Mannering's eyes. He looked as if he might be ready at any moment to plunge into a Rugby scrum.

"If Lorna does this, it will be against my advice," he said flatly.

"I don't care what it's against, but tell Lorna."

"John, I can't speak for Toby Pleydell, but I can tell you in advance that in the opinion of my other partners such a move would be a very grave mistake. If you do it, I doubt whether they would agree to continuing with the defence."

After a long pause, Mannering said levelly: "Just tell Lorna what I want her to do, will you?"

.   .   .   .

"The more I think about it," said Rebecca Blest to Terry McKay, "the more I wonder if those jewels the police showed me this afternoon *were* the same. I thought they were, but—well, I was nervous while I was with that Superintendent Bristow, and wanted to get away."

"The jewels you saw today looked better, perhaps," said Terry McKay.

"The police had probably given them a clean up," said Ruth Ashton.

"That's a thought," McKay said. "Forget it, Becky. Ruth, my pet, *I'll* look after Becky while I'm here. I promise not to be a naughty boy."

"What Becky does about you is up to her," the other girl said tartly. "All I want to be sure is that she's safe. We don't want any more murders."

19

LLOYD DISPOSES

"I simply have to tell you that if you do what John asks I believe it will be a grave mistake," said Lloyd to Lorna.

They were on their own in the flat. Chittering had left before Lloyd had arrived, and Ethel had gone for her evening hour off. "The truth is that John is in a highly emotional state, and he can't hope to assess the situation dispassionately. I know all about his compulsive drive. I can guess what he would do if he were out of prison. But he isn't. I tell you that if this advertisement should ever appear, if claimants came forward for the reward and were proved to have lied, then it would take away one of the most important factors of the defence. John overlooks the fact that the police can't prove there *wasn't* a car here on Tuesday night. In his defence, we can say that it isn't established that no one brought Farmer, that the lack of witnesses in itself is by no means conclusive. We need that element of doubt very badly indeed, and a single false claimant to the reward could kill it."

"I don't see why," Lorna objected.

"It must be obvious! This reward, any reward of such magnitude, is an open invitation for false statements, and the prosecution would make a lot of play on it—arguing that you were virtually bribing people to come forward and perjure themselves. And if we got witnesses to come forward in this way, we might not be able to prove if they were lying, but counsel might when he got them in the witness box. I tell you that it's a very grave risk indeed, and you ought to persuade John to drop it."

Lorna said: "I see what you mean. Yes. Would it—?" she broke off. "All right, Geoff. I'll think about it."

"I wish you'd see a doctor and get a sedative," grumbled Lloyd. "You look tired out."

"I'm all right," Lorna said flatly. The telephone rang, and she was glad of the interruption, for she knew exactly how John had felt. Somehow this reward suggestion would be the kind to appeal to his sense of the dramatic—and he would feel frustrated to a point of exasperation by Lloyd's clinical attitude of disapproval. "Excuse me." She went across to the telephone. "Hallo . . . Oh, good evening, Mr. Entwhistle!"

For a moment, hope surged.

"I'm afraid I haven't had any luck," Entwhistle reported, brisk as always. "But I shall keep on trying, and so will everyone I saw tonight. They're solidly behind Mr. Mannering, you can be sure of that."

"You're very good," Lorna said. "*Very* many thanks for calling. Good night."

"Don't worry too much," urged Entwhistle.

Don't worry too *much*—

"It was a neighbour," Lorna told Lloyd. "They're all being very kind." She spoke mechanically, and did not feel that she could talk in any other way to Lloyd just now; she almost disliked the solicitor. "Everyone is. Geoffrey, I really must try to get some rest."

Lloyd was obviously aware that her mood towards him had changed, that she wanted him to go. He hesitated before turning towards the door, then swung round again in his forceful way, and said:

"Lorna, you may hate my guts at this moment, but I'm advising you for the best. You don't seem to understand—John could hang for these murders."

Lorna stood very still; shocked.

"These *murders*?"

"Yes, murders. You don't need to be told there are the two," said Lloyd, almost desperately. "Whoever hit the man Farmer also hit and killed Samuel Blest. John could have—"

"He wasn't anywhere near the flat!"

"Perhaps he wasn't, but can he prove it? He had been out that afternoon. Samuel Blest was last seen alive just after two, and was found dead at five. John could have gone out to Notting Hill and killed him, and got back in plenty of time to see the girl Rebecca at Quinns."

"Geoffrey," said Lorna, quietly. "I don't think you're the right man to be defending John."

"For God's sake cut out this emotional nonsense and see this as a cold legal problem!" Lloyd almost shouted, and he drew nearer her, one quivering hand raised. "John was out. I haven't asked him directly, but I've asked him in roundabout ways, and he can't establish where he was that afternoon. He went to three or four auction rooms and second-hand shops in the Portobello Road area, but only looked in the windows of some of them. And he travelled by bus and taxi; he didn't take the car because of parking difficulties. I tell you that the prosecution could turn this into a capital murder charge, and if they did that and John was found guilty, he would hang." When Lorna didn't answer, but stood there, shocked beyond words, Lloyd went on: "Why won't you admit that I'm doing my absolute best, that I've got a feeling about this case, and I think it's going wrong. We've got to have the strongest defence we possibly can. If the police catch us out in a single act which looks as if we're trying to buy John off—my God, it will finish him."

"I see, Geoffrey. When are you planning to see John again?"

"Tomorrow morning."

"Well, don't go," Lorna said. "I'll send someone else. I'll tell him that you're ill, if that will make you feel better, but I don't want you to see John again, and I don't want you to handle this case any longer."

"Now, Lorna—"

"There isn't anything to argue about," Lorna said. "I don't believe that anyone who is so sure that John killed these men can possibly help him."

"That's damnably unfair."

"It's damnable all right," Lorna said. "Will you go, please?"

Lloyd started to speak again, then turned round and clumped out; the door closed with a snap. Lorna heard his footsteps on the landing, then on the passage and the stairs; they faded. She felt clammy cold, and frightened. When at last she turned away, she asked herself in a low-pitched voice: "What on earth's the matter with every-one?" And then: "What's the matter with *me*?"

She shivered. She hated every word that Lloyd had said, but he had put doubt back into her mind, had rekindled the fear which she had felt earlier and had managed to push away. How much of the truth had John told? Could he be caught out in a positive lie? Could the police ever prove, for instance, that he had really put the genuine jewels into his own strong-room? If it could be proved that he had lied to Rebecca Blest about them, the rest of the case would almost certainly go against him.

Had he lied?

"Of course he didn't lie," Lorna told herself savagely. "You're as bad as Lloyd! I hate all lawyers." She went into the empty study, stood looking at John's chair, and choked back a flood of emotion. She went to the chair, sat down, and lifted the telephone; she dialled the *Globe*, and it was a long time before there was any answer. The ringing sound going on and on, as if in a vacuum, was like this case; they could never get anywhere. She knew what John would feel; she knew that he would sense what Lloyd really thought.

"*Daily Globe?*"

"Mr. Chittering, please, in the reporters' room."

"Hold on."

Lorna heard the click of the plugs being connected, and then a noise of a telephone being lifted, but there was no immediate answer, just a hum of voices in the background; someone had lifted the receiver and put it on the desk and continued what he was doing. Frustration, frustration, frustration.

"Hallo?" It *was* Chittering.

"Chitty, are you—"

"Lorna?" Chittering interrupted. "Where are you?"

"At home. Chitty, could you come and—"

"Yes," said Chittering, interrupting again, and Lorna could not understand why he spoke so tersely. "I was coming soon, anyway. Stay in, won't you?"

"Of course."

"I'll see you," Chittering said, and rang off; he sounded as brusque as if he had lost the mood of friendliness. *Chittering?* It was nonsense even to think so. If he turned, as Lloyd had, then it would seem as if some hoodoo was upon them, blighting all hope of getting John free. There couldn't be anything wrong with Chittering, unless—

Unless he had discovered some reason for thinking that John was guilty.

Lorna poured herself a whisky-and-soda, sipped it, lit a cigarette, and moved about the room; she had never felt so lonely or so frightened. Now there was this new menace hanging over her head—hanging over *John's* head. A noose.

She went to the kitchen and got out the coffee things; Chittering always liked coffee. As she stood in the larder, there was a ring at the front door bell. She turned her body and looked towards the door. She was so much on her own, but there were a lot of people whom she did not want to see. Lloyd might have come back, for instance; or the police might be here with more questions.

She wished she was not on her own. When John had last been here by himself and that door bell had rung, he had opened it on to the man reeling against the wall outside.

Hadn't he?

Then why hadn't there been bloodstains on the wall? The bell rang again before she reached the door. She heard a man say: "There's a light, so someone's in." It was an innocent kind of remark, and the voice hadn't the depth of a policeman's, more of a youth's.

She opened the door, and saw Rebecca Blest with a

young, curly-haired lad; two young people, side by side and holding hands.

"Why, good evening," Lorna said. She was surprised but not disappointed, glad that there was no fear of another clash with Lloyd. "Come in." She stood aside, and they entered, looking round quickly, and obviously impressed; when she thought of their background, that wasn't surprising. Lorna hadn't seen McKay before, but she liked the look of him, and now that Rebecca Blest had rested, and was made up a little, she was young and attractive and—honest-looking. It was easy to understand John deciding to help her.

She began: "Mrs. Mannering—"

"Mrs. Mannering—" the youth started at the same moment.

They broke off together.

"I was just making coffee," Lorna said. "Would you like a cup?"

"Well—"

"Look, Mrs. Mannering," the youth said, speaking hastily, "I'm Terence McKay, and I happened to meet Becky on the day that she came to Quinns. I dare say you've heard of me."

They were moving towards John's study.

"I have indeed," Lorna said.

"Well, no one wants to find the murderer of Becky's father more than I do, or Becky does," declared the youth, with the sweeping confidence of the young. "But we'd hate the wrong man to be landed with it."

Lorna said: "Well, so would I." It was impossible to say why, but the arrival and the manner of the couple had soothed her; so did the words. They entered the study, and she sat in John's chair, while the girl stood looking at her from the fireplace, and the youth paced about.

"Well, I don't even know if we ought to be here," said McKay, "but we decided to have a go. You know those jewels that Becky took to your husband?"

"I know the ones you mean."

"Well, the police showed her some jewels today, and asked her to identify them. At the time she said they were the ones which she'd taken to Quinns, but she's been thinking since then, and remembered one or two things. She says that the settings—you know, the gold in which the jewels are set—aren't the same. She couldn't tell a genuine diamond from a piece of glass in a ring, any more than I could, and there was the right number of articles there, if you see what I mean . . ."

Lorna's heart was beginning to pound with new hope.

". . . bracelets, necklaces, brooches, ear-rings, that kind of thing. There were seventeen, and they looked pretty well the same, but Becky says she's sure now that they weren't exactly the same," McKay announced. "Those she saw today looked much better. We've been talking about it, and, well, we thought it was only fair to tell you, so that you can pass it on to your lawyers. Eh, Becky?"

"Yes, of course," Rebecca Blest said. "I would hate any injustice to be done, Mrs. Mannering, and—well, the trouble is, I *did* say they were the same ones. What I wonder is ought I to tell the police I think I was wrong? I remembered how worried you were last night, and I thought I'd like to come and see you, anyhow."

"You couldn't have done a kinder thing," Lorna said. She almost choked. "You—you would really stand up in court and say this?"

"Oh, yes," said Rebecca. "After all, it's the truth."

Thank God for her simplicity!

"Wonderful," Lorna said. "It's wonderful. It's the fact that the police found the jewels in my husband's strong-room which really make them think he—" She broke off, hearing footsteps outside again, and before she finished, there was another *ting* at the front door bell. This would be Chittering. Immediately she wondered whether it would be wise to tell Chittering about this, because he might want to use it in his newspaper, and she could not be sure whether that would help or not.

She needed legal advice, even if it had to be Lloyd's.

"That's a newspaperman from the *Globe*," she said. "Don't say anything about this until I ask you to, will you?"

"Mum's the word," promised McKay.

It would have been easy to laugh, but laughter would have had a touch of hysteria. Lorna went out of the room, and hesitated for a moment, unable to realise the full significance of what she now knew, realising only that this could be the beginning of the end of the chain of misfortunes. She recovered herself and opened the door.

It was Chittering.

The moment she saw him, she knew that he had much on his mind, that she had not been mistaken about the oddness of the way he had talked and his brusqueness on the telephone. He said briskly: "Hallo, Lorna," and stepped inside. "Are you alone? I've some news of a kind that could be important. I don't know just how, yet. It could be a hoax, and—"

He broke off sharply, for McKay appeared in the doorway.

20

HOAX OR OFFER?

"What's this?" demanded Chittering. "You playing detective, too?" There was a sharp note in his voice, but any hint of criticism was killed by the way he smiled at Lorna, and added: "What a lucky man John is!"

"I asked Rebecca Blest to come and see me. If she could spare the time," Lorna improvised, "and Mr. McKay brought her."

"That explains the motor-cycle I saw downstairs," said Chittering. "Any sensations for a newspaper-man?"

"I'm afraid not," said Rebecca, coming into sight.

Chittering spoke as if he were quite satisfied:

"While you're here, then, there's one thing you could help to clear up—not for publication, but to help us get at the facts. Do you know whether entry was forced into your flat when your father was attacked, Miss Blest?" When the girl didn't answer immediately, he went on: "I'm sorry to keep reminding you, but this could be very important. The police have been cagey with me and I don't know whether this means they've got information they don't want me to have, or are cagey about being so ignorant."

McKay said: "It was opened with a key, Becky, wasn't it?"

"Well, I think so," answered the girl. "I remember that the police spread a lot of powder round the key hole. I think they were looking for fingerprints, and I heard someone say that there weren't any, and there weren't any scratches. So it looks as if a key was used."

"Or a skeleton key," put in McKay, eagerly. "Some of these thieves can open a door with a bit of bent wire, and not leave a trace. And I knew a chap once who could open a car door—"

"Friend of yours?" inquired Chittering.

McKay grinned.

"Not exactly, and he's in prison now, but I don't mind admitting that I admired the way he did it, even if I don't approve of thievery. What difference does it make how the door was opened?"

"If by a key, who had keys?" inquired Chittering.

"That's a point," McKay admitted.

Lorna was watching the girl closely. She was anxious to hear what Chittering had come about, and the talk of a hoax had puzzled her; but the youngsters had brought a kind of hope for the first time, and it was possible that they could offer more. Chittering was obviously very anxious to have the answer. The girl frowned in concentration. She looked more tired now than when she had come into the flat, as if she had keyed herself up to the effort, and once it was made she had drooped.

"I had one," she said slowly. "And my father, of course, and—my uncle."

"Rett Laker?" Chittering exclaimed.

"Yes," answered Rebecca. "I've been trying to remember whether we ever got it back after—after his death. I don't think we did."

"It would be worth trying to check," said Chittering, and went on almost casually: "Did you have a key hanging inside the letter box so that if you lost your own, all you had to do was hook the piece of string out and get hold of the key?"

"No. My father was always very insistent that we shouldn't do that."

"Wise chap," said Chittering, and paused. "Well, if you want my opinion, Becky should be getting to bed pretty soon, she looks tired out. Is that bag of bones called Ruth still keeping you company, Becky?" Chittering could get away with a cheeky impudence which a lot of people liked.

"Ruth's been very kind," said Rebecca. "All the Ashtons have, they've been *very* kind. But—"

"Any reason why we shouldn't hear what you came to tell Mrs. Mannering?" demanded McKay, hopefully.

"Yes," answered Chittering, flatly. "A lot of reasons—it's highly confidential."

"Oh, well—I tried," said McKay. "We'd better get along."

"Mrs. Mannering," Rebecca said, with appealing sincerity, "I hope very much that you can prove that your husband is innocent."

Lorna just managed to say: "Thank you." She went to the door with them, and watched them walking down the stairs; before they were half-way down the first flight, their hands were clutching. Chittering was standing at Lorna's shoulder, and as she turned away and closed the door, he said:

"That looks like a case of young love."

"I hope it is," said Lorna. "That child needs someone to help her. Has she any relatives?"

"None we've heard of, and none the police have traced," answered Chittering. Obviously he was still suppressing his excitement, but doing so more effectively than before. He led the way into the kitchen, the door of which stood open, and sniffed. Lorna heard the percolator bubbling. "What did that couple come for?"

Lorna said resignedly: "So you weren't fooled."

"Of course I wasn't. Not for my ears?"

"I didn't want them to know that you knew," said Lorna. "It must be confidential, Chitty."

"Lorna, my dear," said Chittering, turning to face her, and putting his hands on her shoulders, "I have one interest and one interest only: getting John cleared. I shall use nothing in the *Globe* that might do him the slightest harm. I'm on your side all the way. You know that, don't you?"

"Yes," said Lorna, in a muffled voice. "Yes, of course I do. But—"

"I know about the row with Lloyd," Chittering went on. "He telephoned me just after he left here, and asked me to plead for him. I hedged. We can talk about that afterwards. It's still possible that Toby Pleydell will be here in the morning, and that will get us out of the legal hiatus. What did the young innocents want—*if* they're innocents?"

Lorna told him.

After a pause, Chittering said softly: "Well, well, a hole in the police case after all. If Becky will say in court that she thinks the jewellery she gave John and the jewellery shown to her by the police and offered as Exhibit A wasn't the same, then—well, Lloyd would have a bit more of the defence evidence he wants."

"Chitty—"

"I know, I know," said Chittering hastily. "We are not going to allow the case to get to a trial, we want a 'case dismissed' decision next Wednesday, or else a withdrawal of the charges. I think Lloyd's probably right to try the coldly pessimistic attitude, but that's by the way. A very peculiar thing happened tonight."

Lorna didn't speak.

"Happened to me," went on Chittering, in an over-stilted voice. "I'd been out on the case, the editor having assigned me to it full time, and I was trying to get something from the other people who live in Larraby's mews, about other people being there on Tuesday night. No luck, so far. There never were so many people who heard nothing. I was waylaid by a man coming away from the mews, and he told me that if I wanted to help one John Mannering, I should telephone a certain number. This number," Chittering added, and drew a slip of paper out of his pocket. He showed the pencilled letters and figures to Lorna; the number was PADDINGTON 92543.

"Did you ring it?"

"I did, from the nearest call box," Chittering replied. "I got an answer after a long, long time. A man answered." He paused, as if he found it difficult to say what the message was, and Lorna fought back her impatience, yet felt her nerves more on edge than ever. "It shook me badly."

"Chitty—"

"The man said that for a sufficient reward, he would give me the name of witnesses who could help. He said that these witnesses could prove that Farmer had been attacked before he came up to the flat—in a car in Green Street, in fact. In other words, he certainly knows enough about the case to realise what evidence John needs, and how badly we need it. But—"

"But *what*?"

"It could be a hoax," Chittering said reasoningly. "It could be a clever way of getting some easy money, too. He wants a thousand pounds for the information."

Lorna echoed: "A *thou*sand."

"A thousand pounds for what might be a simple fraud," said Chittering. "I doubt if we'll know whether it is or not unless the money is paid over. I am to be one messenger. You are to come with me."

Lorna said: "If it were ten thousand it would be worth it even for half a chance. Did—did Lloyd tell you about John's reward suggestion?"

"Yes."

Lorna said, slowly: "And you don't think it's a good one, either."

"From John, hopeless. But if the *Globe* offered the reward, it would be a different kettle of fish," Chittering pointed out quietly. "I doubt if the old rag would go to ten thousand, but it would go to one or two. What are we going to do about this message?"

"We're going to take a chance," Lorna said at once. "We must."

"I suppose so," agreed Chittering, a little uneasily. "We can sleep on it, anyhow—we're to go and see this man tomorrow evening, after dark."

"Where?"

"We're to meet him at Hammersmith Underground Station," answered Chittering. "He will come up to us, and in exchange for the money, give us more details. It sounds preposterous, but—"

"We've got to do it."

"Lloyd wouldn't agree."

"I don't care what Lloyd thinks," Lorna said. "Chitty, we need another lawyer, who—"

"Listen, my dear," Chittering interrupted. He reminded her very much of Lloyd in that moment, and she felt almost antagonistic towards him. "If John swops lawyers, it will hit all the headlines. It will prove complete lack of trust between him and Lloyd, and make it extremely difficult for Toby Pleydell to take over. I think you've got to wait a bit before you decide what to do, at least until Toby arrives. And he'll be here, there's no more doubt of that."

"How can you be sure?"

"His plane left Idlewild at half-past nine, Greenwich Mean Time." Chittering told her, and for the second time tonight she felt a flare of hope. "He'll be here at crack of dawn. So will I, and we can have a long session and work out policy before he goes to see John. But there's one other thing."

"Yes?"

"You mustn't leave here," said Chittering. "And you mustn't take any notice of any messages you might get. You and John are both too emotionally involved, you're not seeing really straight. God knows I don't blame you, but it's something you've both got to realise."

21

FRIEND

"HALLO, John," Toby Pleydell said. "Sorry I'm late."

He came into the cell at Brixton, tall, lean, a Punch of a man with a hooked nose and greying hair, about Mannering's age, and a friend of his since schooldays. Socially, they had everything in common. Sight of Pleydell did Mannering more good than anything had for the past three days.

They gripped hands as the warder closed and locked the door behind him.

"Thanks for rushing," Mannering said. "I'm sorry to be a damned nuisance."

"Don't be an ass," said Pleydell. He took off his top coat, draped it over a chair, and took out cigarettes in a gold case. He looked immaculate, and quite fresh, in spite of the long flight. "One or two preliminaries first. I've had a talk with Lloyd, and of course I'm taking over completely."

"Lloyd doesn't exactly fill me with confidence," said Mannering. "Does he think I used the hammer?"

"He thinks the police might be able to build up a case which would be hard to beat. And he's half right, too—about the reward, for instance. We mustn't offer it, but I could swing the *Globe* to, and that would let you out."

Mannering sat on an upright chair, smiled tautly, and nodded:

"So you've also been talking to Chitty."

"We had a breakfast session with Lorna," said Pleydell. "Can't understand her, she wants you back!" He waited for a moment, before going on: "I think I'm bang up to date with the whole situation, and there are only a few things which you don't yet know. Entry into Blest's flat, for the murder, was by key or skeleton key—that's firmly established. The picture taken from Larraby's place is still missing, and no one has any idea where to look for it. Larraby's improving, but still in the nursing home, and his memory is still a complete blank. I haven't seen him, but Lorna has, and he's heard what's happened. Lorna says that he's almost distraught."

"He would be," said Mannering, slowly.

"There's still no word about anyone seen in Green Street about the time Farmer came to see you," said Pleydell, "except one thing, which isn't really any help."

Mannering's eyes brightened.

"Go on."

"Last night, Chittering had a telephone call," said Pleydell, and he told Mannering exactly what Chittering had told Lorna, going into precise details. Mannering first felt a sense of shock, which gradually turned into excitement. He clenched his hands on the table between him and Pleydell, and fought against interrupting. Pleydell managed to make the scene near the mews vivid, and made no comment, just recited the bare facts.

Mannering said: "So it's beginning."

"What do you mean?"

"There had to be a motive for it all. It's beginning to show."

"You mean—" Pleydell began.

"I mean that sooner or later there had to be a demand of some kind, and this looks like the start of it," said Mannering. Excitement and bitterness welled up and warred inside him. He jumped to his feet, knowing that the warder outside the door could hear, and cried: "If only I were out of this bloody place, if only I could go and talk to this man!"

"Keep quiet!" Pleydell said sharply.

"Quiet? Toby, don't even you understand? It's all coming out, now. This is a form of blackmail, and this move is the beginning of it."

"It could well be a hoax."

"Does it sound like a hoax?"

"Now listen, John—"

"All right, all right," said Mannering, and dropped back on to the chair. The feeling of frustration which had caused the eruption was a little less acute, but he knew that he was wrong to give way to it, that Pleydell was right to make a rational approach. "It could be a hoax, but it doesn't sound like one to me. It sounds like the beginning of the squeeze. One thousand pounds, for introduction to a man who could save me. Then the introduction. Then another demand. Then—"

"You're only guessing."

"Oh, yes," agreed Mannering. "I'm only guessing, but when Lorna has seen this chap, it will be more than guessing."

"You want her to?"

Mannering stared. "Of course."

"Isn't there grave danger for her?"

Mannering said: "Even you, Toby? Is Lorna the only one who can see this as I do?" He leaned across the table, and went on evenly: "Listen, old chap—there isn't anything else to do. This job has been very cleverly handled, even brilliantly handled. The other side has judged this call to perfection—at a time when Lorna and I are bound to be stretched pretty taut, but while there's still time for us to believe that we can save the situation. As for danger—of course there isn't any physical danger for Lorna."

"You can't be sure."

"But if anything were to happen to Lorna, how could this unknown man get his hands on any money? Who but Lorna will pay for this kind of information? Lorna's absolutely safe while she appears to be willing to do what this man wants. If she refuses, if she tries any tricks, if the police were to watch when she goes to the rendezvous, then there would be plenty of danger. But the man's so clever that he wants her to take Chittering. He isn't asking her to go alone, which would practically make her tell the police and ask for their protection. She'll be as safe as houses. If there's danger, it will come later."

Pleydell said: "I wish I could be so sure, but I'll tell Lorna."

"Toby."

"Yes?"

"Only Lorna. Not the police."

"Only Lorna and Chittering," Pleydell promised.

"Thanks," said Mannering. "Thanks." After a moment or two, he went on: "Now—what else is there?" He began to walk about the room, trying to get this last crisis out of his mind, trying to remember everything else that Pleydell had told him. "Entrance to Samuel Blest's flat by key . . . no trace of the coloured man who picked up the messages for Klein at the Overseas Club . . . no trace of that picture. Why steal that picture? Why break the glass?" He paused again, but only for a moment. "That's about it, and no one could say it was very much. Nothing else at all?"

Pleydell said: "One thing, John, which could help a lot."

"Now come on," urged Mannering. "Why hold out on me?" He felt his heart hammering. "Good news of a kind, then?"

"Rebecca Blest isn't sure that the jewels the police showed her are the ones which she brought to you," Pleydell announced.

Mannering stared. "Rebecca says *that*?" He sat down again, feeling too numbed for excitement. "So, she isn't sure. She doesn't hate. She'll say that in court although it might help me to get off?"

"She'll say it."

"Toby," Mannering said, "for the first time I think things might work out. I really think they might. Go and see Lorna right away, won't you?"

"Straight from here," promised Pleydell.

Mannering watched him go.

He noticed every movement and everything about Pleydell. They were of a height too. Pleydell stood by the door, and called out: "I'm ready." It was a voice which Mannering could imitate without difficulty. He stood to one side. When the door opened, the warder would appear and look straight up at him—that was the moment of danger for the warder, and for Mannering if he tried to escape. It would be easy, up to a point. He could over-power Toby and could change into his clothes. He could wait for that warder, deal with the man, and get outside. And then? It might be difficult, but it could be done. Everyone would be expecting Pleydell, remember—a tall, lean man.

Was it madness?

"John," Pleydell said, before the door opened. "I've never known the police so watchful. They've got special men posted at all the gates of the prison."

It was almost as if he could read Mannering's thoughts; and, in a way, he could almost certainly guess at them. He had known Mannering for so many years, there were inevitable and specific trains of thought in such circum-stances.

"Is that so?" Mannering made himself say.

"It's so."

"Thanks," said Mannering.

"Ready, sir?" asked the warder.

"Yes," said Pleydell. He smiled and waved, then went out quickly. As the door closed, Mannering said softly:

"You cunning old fox!" He gave a high-pitched laugh, and that in itself told him how worked up he was; how little things affected him—and now there was much more than a little thing: there was good reason for hope. If Rebecca Blest testified that she wasn't sure of the identity of the jewels, it could be the beginning of the end of the prosecution's case. Long live—

"My God!" breathed Mannering, and his voice rose. He ran to the door and banged on it. "*Warder!*" The man wasn't in earshot; he was letting Pleydell out of the door along the end of the passage. "*Warder!*" he shouted again, and there came a brief pause, followed by footsteps. He stood back as the warder opened the door; another man was with him, as if to corroborate Pleydell's warning of the powerful watch. "Sorry," choked Mannering, "but see if you can get Mr. Pleydell back for me, will you?"

"I think we'll be able to catch him," the warder said. "Just to make sure, I'll phone a message through to the gates."

.   .   .   .

"Toby," Mannering said urgently, "look after Rebecca Blest. She's a vital witness. See that she comes to no harm. If the other side knows what she's prepared to say in court, then they might think she's better dead."

.   .   .   .

Rebecca got up a little after nine o'clock that morning, her eyes rather heavy, her heart heavy as it always was on the first moment of waking, and of realisation. The little bedroom was chilly, and she shivered as she crossed to the bathroom. Ruth Ashton had been sleeping up here with her, and must have been gone for half an hour or more. She normally left the house at twenty past eight, to get to her typing job in the West End by nine o'clock. It was very cold. Rebecca switched on the electric fire, and made some tea. She went back to her bedroom with it, switched on the fire there, sat on the bed with her feet dangling before it, and said:

"It's time I went back to work!"

She wouldn't be going back until the day after tomorrow, for tomorrow was the day of the funeral. She wished that it was over. She hated the prospect, and until it was over she would feel dreadful. Yet, quite honest with herself, she admitted that there were already moments when she forgot. Once or twice last night, for instance, when she had been with Terry. Her heart was lighter even now, at thought of him. He could make her laugh, he could make her smile, above all he could make her feel that she was wanted, that she was not really alone in the world. The feeling of loneliness since her father's death had in some ways been worse than anything else.

When it was all over, she and Terry—

She allowed herself to day-dream, although at the back of her mind there was the realisation that there might be no justification for such dreams. They had known each other only a few days, and although he was kindliness itself, Terry might just be feeling great pity for her, and only be anxious to help. Yet there were moments when she felt that he already thought much more of her than that.

It was nearly ten o'clock.

"My goodness!" she exclaimed. She jumped up, hurried into the kitchen with the tray, then went and washed, dressed and made up. By the time she had finished it was half-past ten, and she was very hungry.

The ordinary sounds of the street floated in, including children shouting, but she hardly noticed them. She made some toast; it was years since she had cooked a full breakfast, except on Sundays. She sat in the kitchen overlooking the back yard, and the backs of the houses in another street like this. Three lines of washing were hanging so motionless that this would obviously be a bad drying day. She had a few smalls to wash herself, but they could dry in the kitchen. Tears suddenly welled up in her eyes; there would be no more washing for her father.

Why had this terrible thing happened?

She was standing there, with her eyes filled with tears, when she heard a sound. She didn't think much about it at first, for sounds travelled clearly in this house, and noises across the landing often seemed as if they were in the flat itself. She kept seeing an image of her father's face, and fighting back emotion.

She heard another sound; a rustling.

For the first time, she was startled and a little scared. She looked towards the door, but nothing moved. She didn't hear the sound again, but it was almost as if someone was moving along the passage. She made herself get up. Her heart was beating faster than usual, and she was breathing more quickly, too.

It must be nonsense!

The front door was closed. The other doors were ajar, except that of her father's bedroom. It had been imagination, of course; she hadn't heard a sound of any kind except from the street. Trying to reassure herself, she went across to her bedroom and pushed the door open cautiously. It didn't go right back against the wall, but she didn't realise that was significant. She went into the room—and heard a sound again, just behind her, *close* behind her. She swung round. She saw a man leaping forward, his hand raised, a hammer in it. His face was hidden by a mask, his head covered with a cloth cap, and he wore a big, shapeless overcoat. She screamed:

"No!"

She struck out blindly, and pulled at the door; and it was the door which got in his way, so that he smashed the hammer against the wood. She heard him swear.

She rushed out into the passage, gasping for breath, trying to scream but unable to make much noise. She reached the front door and snatched at the latch, but she missed it, and tore a finger-nail. She was gabbling to herself: "Oh God, dear God, help me, help me!" She heard a door bang, and at the same time she heard a shout from outside. She screamed again—and this time it was a piercing shriek which seemed to deafen her. She tried the door again as footsteps sounded on the stairs, and a man cried out:

"All right, I'm coming! I'm coming!"

She turned round. The man with the scarf over his face was standing only a few feet away from her, the hammer still in his hand; and she knew that if he struck her with it, she would die. She felt sure that this was the man who had killed her father.

"*No, no, no!*" she screamed.

"Open the door!" cried the man outside. "Open it!"

The man struck at her with the hammer, and in wild

fear she kicked at him. His blow missed, and she heard him gasp with pain. Then he swung round and ran away, limping, towards the kitchen. As he disappeared, slamming the door, she began to sob.

She was still sobbing when she opened the door to Tom Wainwright, from Quinns. It was too late to give chase, then.

22

DEADLY RISK

MANNERING heard footsteps outside the door, and stood up. It was nearly one o'clock. Two people were coming, besides the warder, and he tried to recognise the footsteps. Pleydell's? As the door opened, the keys clanking, he recalled them: Pleydell's and Bristow's. Pleydell came in first, with a "Hallo, John". Bristow followed. Bristow had a freshly-shaved, freshly-dressed look, and his gardenia was glowing white. The door closed behind them.

"Good morning, Superintendent," Mannering said.

" 'Morning, John," returned Bristow.

"All friends together again, are we?"

"I'm a policeman and you're a man accused of murder," Bristow said. "So don't expect me to apologise because I fully agreed with the charge."

"And don't you now?"

Pleydell said: "You're an uncanny devil, John. You were right about the danger to Rebecca Blest."

Mannering felt a flare of alarm.

"Is she all right?"

"Thanks to you, she is," said Pleydell. "And thanks to the fact that the moment I told young Tom, he went haring off to Notting Hill, and got there in time to . . ." Pleydell told Tom's story, and Bristow nodded agreement from time to time.

Mannering sat back on the upright chair, leaning on the two back legs, understanding a great deal, believing that he understood the reason for Bristow's friendlier manner. But there was an undercurrent of anxiety in Bristow's manner, and in Pleydell's. Both these men had come to try to bring some pressure to bear. There was deep irony in that, and he wondered anxiously what they were after.

". . . so what it amounts to is that Tom did what you would have done had you been free," went on Pleydell. "He probably got there five minutes later than you would have. Incidentally, I also telephoned the Yard, and they arrived five minutes after Tom."

"Five minutes too late," Mannering murmured.

"That's true enough," admitted Bristow. "The girl would have been murdered if your man hadn't got there so soon. Why were you so sure that she was in danger?"

"Don't you know?"

"I've had a talk with her," said Bristow, thoughtfully. "She seems to know what she's about. She's told me that although she formally identified the jewels in my office yesterday, she had doubts afterwards."

"Then you know why I knew she was in danger."

"Was that the only reason?"

"Listen, Bill," Mannering said tautly. "This girl could have broken the police case. My counsel had only to prove one error to make a big crack in the prosecution, and you know it. These people don't want any cracks unless they make them themselves."

Bristow put his head on one side. "I still don't know what you're getting at, and I don't believe I've been told the whole story. I know that Lloyd and you quarrelled, presumably because he wouldn't do something you wanted, and I know that you've been talking to him and to Pleydell very freely. I can well believe that you've been conducting the investigation from here, and I've no objection if your agents keep within the law, but—if I don't know the full facts, I can't help you."

"Bill, so far all you've done is help to get me convicted of murder," Mannering said softly. "I don't think I've any reason to trust any policeman over this, and particularly not you or Ingleby."

"That's reasonable enough," Bristow admitted. "But the fact remains that if there's urgently needed evidence, we are the only people likely to find it quickly enough to help you. If we have any grounds for withdrawing the charges next Wednesday, we'll withdraw them. But if you take risks with other people—if you try directing dangerous operations by remote control, you'll run bang into more trouble."

Mannering looked at Pleydell.

"Toby?"

"He's at least half right," Pleydell conceded.

"How much have you told him?"

"Nothing more than the fact that you saw danger to the girl the moment you heard about her doubts of the jewellery."

"But I know there's something else," Bristow insisted. "I've talked to Lorna. I've talked to Chittering. I've even tried to make your maid talk. And all I get are evasions and half-truths. If you really want to help yourself, do it through us."

Mannering thrust both hands deep into his pockets, and leaned precariously back on the legs of the chair. He studied Bristow's eyes, the clear, light grey eyes of a man he knew to be of great integrity, but in his mind he also saw Ingleby and the other policemen who had watched when he had left the Yard for the court. He realised that he was bitter; very bitter indeed. He also realised that bitterness would not help him; only a calm assessment of the circumstances could. Within the limits of his ability and Scotland Yard regulations, Bristow would now try to uncover the evidence which would save him, but—would Ingleby really work all out on it? Would any of the others? Hadn't the Yard already prejudged him?

And if they hadn't—what would happen if the police were to go tonight to see this man who had talked to Chittering? If he were a practised criminal, and so far he seemed to be outstandingly able, he would soon realise that the police were watching. From the moment he believed that the police were after him, the whole situation would change. Lorna would be in acute danger, while rather than allow himself to be caught, the man might allow him, Mannering, to be tried and convicted.

So, would it be wise, would it even be safe, to confide in the police?

He said: "Toby, just confirm one thing for me, will you? Everything I've told you is in absolute confidence."

"Yes, of course."

"I'd like it to stay that way," Mannering decided.

"Now—" Bristow began.

"Quite sure?" asked Pleydell, where Lloyd would have raised his voice and told him that he was taking grave risks with his own future.

"Yes."

Bristow said, slowly: "John, you're making a big mistake. I can imagine how bitter you're feeling, and I don't blame you. I believed from the beginning that you were trying to help this girl Blest, and up to one of your Sir Galahading tricks, and I wasn't prepared to stand by while you were dealing with the jewels which Rett Laker stole. Remember that these particular jewels in our possession aren't more than a tenth of the whole. We want them all, and we want to catch Laker's accomplices as well as the murderer. But now that serious doubt has been thrown on the identity of the jewels brought to you, I'm prepared to rethink the situation. There are puzzling features about Larraby's condition and the medical opinion is that he had been drugged with amytal. In short, your contention that the real jewels were planted at Quinns so as to involve you seems to have supporting evidence. If that's established, we shall have a completely new situation. And this very morning, murder was attempted. There isn't a lot of time to lose. I want to know everything you can tell me, and you'll be making a grave mistake if you don't come across at once."

Mannering considered for a few moments, then said deliberately:

"No, Bill. Not this time."

Bristow looked at Pleydell. "Try to make him change his mind," he said, and turned to the door. He glanced back but didn't speak again, and Mannering studied his set face as he went out. The door closed behind him, and his footsteps sounded clearly in the passage.

Mannering felt very warm, and his forehead was clammy. There really was the possibility that he had made a grave mistake, and he had to remind himself that he was not taking a personal risk—this time, it was Lorna's.

How great was it?

"I've a message from Lorna," Pleydell said, as Bristow's footsteps faded. "She wants to make the attempt tonight. Chittering will be all ready for trouble."

"Aren't you convinced that I'm crazy?" demanded Mannering.

Pleydell smiled faintly as he looked hard at his friend, and it was a long time before he answered. While waiting, Mannering felt a fresh disquiet of doubt creep into his mind. Again he felt the almost desperate longing to be outside, to handle the situation for himself; but it was an unattainable yearning.

"Well?" he asked sharply.

"John," Pleydell said, "you've been at this kind of game for a long time. No one knows that more than Lorna and me. You've got a kind of sixth sense about the right thing to do. Bristow knows that, and thinks it might pay off, or he wouldn't have given up so easily. He's done his duty, and that's as far as he will go. I think that you're almost certainly right to try to handle this without the police, and Lorna and Chittering agree. There may come a time when they'll have to go to the Yard, but that's for an emergency." Pleydell paused, before he added: "I've only one real worry."

Mannering was feeling much, much better.

"What is it?"

"What would probably succeed if you were handling it yourself, might fail because Lorna and Chittering won't be able to sum up the situation as quickly, and won't be able to work under pressure as well as you do."

"I know," said Mannering, heavily. "I know. Lorna's behind me?"

"A hundred per cent."

"Toby, I think they ought to go tonight," Mannering decided. "And I still think Lorna will be safe enough, provided only Chittering goes with her. The risk will come if the police follow, or if Tom or anyone else shows up. The police might follow Lorna and Chittering, without saying what they mean to do. If there's any evidence of it, call the whole thing off. Is that clear? Lorna and Chittering must go alone."

"I'll see that they do," promised Pleydell.

When the solicitor had gone, Mannering sat back on the chair, with his head resting against the wall, his eyes closed, his lips set tightly. Everything that had been said passed through his mind, as though it were a fine mesh screen. He could imagine all the risks, and all the chances of failure. Out there by himself, he was sure that he could have coped. Could the others? Was there any reasonable hope that they could?

He felt sure of only one thing: if the police went with Lorna and Chittering, or if they followed, and the criminal found out, that would be the end of the chance. Bristow had put his finger on the weakness of his own case. The murderer and those working with him still had the rest of the stolen jewellery. At the first real threat of danger, they would fade out, and hold on to the jewellery for a long time before trying to dispose of it.

The obvious fact crept up on Mannering as he sat there, his mind roaming over the whole of London—so obvious that it could easily be overlooked.

The key to this affair was the fact that someone had nearly half a million pounds worth of precious stones. What could they want him to do—except sell it for them?

.   .   .   .

Every time Lorna caught sight of a policeman, that night, she wondered if the man would report to the Yard that he had recognised her. Every time a man appeared to be following her too closely, she wondered if it was a plainclothes man. Even at Hammersmith Broadway Underground Station, where a trickle of people went in and out, she felt that she was being watched.

Chittering was near her, but they had not arrived together.

Lorna was wearing a cloth coat and a beret, and carrying a handbag with a shoulder strap, with the thousand pounds in notes. Nothing could prevent her from looking distinctive, but no one would have suspected her tension or her nervousness. Most men who passed glanced at her.

It was nine-fifteen; the time that Chittering had been told to bring her here.

She saw him now, standing by the ticket machines further inside the station. He did not make any sign, but kept looking her way. She walked about, to try to ease the tension, and was facing the interior of the station—and Chittering—when she heard a crash just outside. She turned, in alarm. A woman cried out: "*Oo look!*" Two cars had collided, the front of one with the back of another, and a cyclist had been thrown to the ground. In that instant, a crowd seemed to rise from out of the pavement, and two policemen appeared as if by magic and went to the spot. Lorna found herself tempted to go nearer, resisted the temptation, turned round and looked for Chittering.

He wasn't in sight.

He had been, only a few seconds before.

Where on earth—?

A man came up behind her, took her arm, making her jump in alarm, and said into her ear:

"Walk straight on, Mrs. Mannering. We are going to take a short ride by tube, and then by car to a place where we will meet a certain Mr. Smith."

Lorna heard the deep, low-pitched voice, glanced round, and saw the dark face of the man by her side, noticed the dark fingers gripping her arm. This was a coloured man, stocky, powerful, knowing exactly what he was about. He led the way towards the barrier, showed two tickets, kept his hand on her arm, and went on:

"You'll be all right, Mrs. Mannering, if you do what you're told. You won't come to any harm. You just do what you're told, ma'am. Mr. Smith's a man of his word."

23

MOTIVE

LORNA went down the staircase to the platform, stepped into a train which drew in noisily, and got out at Earl's Court, when the coloured man touched her arm. She felt numbed. There was no sign of Chittering, no indication that she had been followed. She stepped on to the platform at Earl's Court, and the coloured man said:

"Now listen carefully, Mrs. Mannering, and do exactly what you are told. Go to the main exit, and just wait there. A man from a dark blue Vauxhall car will come for you. Will you recognise a blue Vauxhall?"

"Yes."

"That man will take you to Mr. Smith," the coloured man said. He gripped her arm as if he had not yet finished, and lowered his voice: "Just one question, ma'am. You haven't been followed by the police, have you?"

"No," Lorna said, stiffly. "That was agreed."

"That's good, that's very good," the coloured man said. "Mr. Smith wouldn't like it if the police were following you. Good night, ma'am."

He let her go, and she still had the money.

She walked slowly towards the foot of the steps. A dozen or so passengers had got out of the train, and most were waiting to change to another line. She went up the steps. No one appeared to take any notice of her, and there was no sign of Chittering. A uniformed policeman at the exit was standing about and rubbing his hands together; he took no notice of her. Several other people were standing and waiting, and a young couple just in front of her were nuzzling each other. The policeman turned and strolled off. As soon as he was out of sight, a man came from one side and ranged himself by Lorna.

"Got the money?"

"Yes," she said.

"Hand it over then."

"When I've got the information," Lorna said.

"Just give me the money, and follow me," the man ordered.

What would John do in these circumstances? That was the pressing, urgent question on Lorna's mind.

She gave the man the bag and he looked inside. She was afraid he would just walk off, but instead he said:

"This way."

He led her fifty yards along the road, to a dark coloured car; a Vauxhall. She could not see his face properly, for his coat collar was turned up. He was a man of medium height, and white-skinned. He opened the door of the car, waited for her to get in, then joined her. A man at the wheel started off immediately.

Lorna knew the district reasonably well, and knew that they were heading for the Paddington area, but before long they turned into a side street. The driver hadn't spoken. All she could see was the back of his head, and his shoulders. The street was dark, with only one lamp burning. She began to feel terribly afraid, but made no comment, and stared straight ahead. The driver went out of this street, then turned corner after corner; she felt sure that he was checking whether they were being followed. Finally he pulled up by a stretch of waste land, where buildings had been demolished. Across the patch of land there were blocks of flats with many lighted windows, but they seemed a long way off.

It was lonely here, and deserted, and her fears grew into dread.

The driver said:

"You got the money?"

"Yes," the man answered.

"Checked her for a tape-recorder?"

"No."

"Well, check."

Lorna steeled herself against the touch of the man's hands, as he patted her clothes and felt inside her pockets. Finally, he gave her back the empty bag, and said:

"She's clean."

"Good. Now, we needn't be long, Mrs. Mannering," said the driver. "Why didn't you bring the police?"

"Because—" she broke off. "Because my husband advised against it."

"Mannering did? How come?"

"He sent me word through his solicitor."

"So he did," said the man at the wheel, with deep satisfaction. He did not turn his head, but she could see that his ear was white, too. He had a powerful voice, with a touch of Cockney, vaguely familiar because of that Cockney twang. He wore a dark trilby hat, pulled low over his forehead, and was muffled with a scarf as if this were a bitter winter's night. "He's no fool, I'll say that for him, and he's used to taking risks. Well, he can clear himself of this trouble if he'll take enough risks—*and* if you'll join him in them."

Lorna didn't speak.

The man said: "Farmer was going to do a deal with Mannering. He was going to tell him what I was planning, and he reckoned Mannering would see him right. Well, someone else saw him right. I was waiting for him when he came to Green Street, and his skull wasn't as thick as he thought it was. It nearly was—he lived longer than I meant him to, but not too long. You could do with a witness to swear that Farmer was hurt before he got to Green Street, couldn't you?"

Lorna almost choked. "Yes."

"I can find him," the man said. "I can find three reputable citizens who will come forward and clear Mannering. They will be able to stand up to any interrogation, and the police will have to drop the charge. It's that easy. And don't make any mistake, Mrs. Mannering —I made sure no one else could give this kind of evidence. It's my witnesses or none at all."

Lorna asked: "And what does my husband have to do to—to make sure of their testimony?"

"Good question," said the driver, still looking straight ahead. "In fact, that's the key question, Mrs. Mannering. He has to find three hundred thousand pounds, and see that I get it in cash. He can still make a good profit—because he's got to buy Rett Laker's jewellery with the money. I've been waiting for that stuff for fifteen years. I waited until Laker came out of prison, then I did a deal with him, and got my hands on the jewellery at last. But it wasn't any use to me without a good market, and I'd got my market all prepared. Quinns, that's my market. I once thought Mannering would buy it straight, knowing it was hot, but Laker *alias* Klein checked on that and we decided it wouldn't work. We started to try Mannering out again through the girl, but—"

The man by Lorna's side said: "You don't have to tell the story of your life."

"Okay," said the driver, after a short pause. "Okay, I don't. Mrs. Mannering, Quinns has got to buy the jewellery for three hundred thousand pounds, in one go. Quinns can find the money. I know its financial strength. The stuff's dangerous to me. I want to get rid of it, but I don't want to use the ordinary fences—they'd try to chisel, or they'd squeak. So Mannering's risk is having stolen jewellery to dispose of, that's all. If he's forced to it, he won't find it so difficult, and I never knew the man who would give up a hundred-and-fifty thousand pounds to keep his hands clean."

Smith stopped.

The man by Lorna's side said: "You heard him, didn't you?"

"Yes," Lorna said. "Yes, I heard him." She hesitated before asking: "What guarantee is there that the witnesses will come forward?"

"You don't get any guarantee," said the driver. "But they'll come forward all right. If they don't, you'll tell the police the whole story, and the hunt will be up. I don't want that. I want a nice quiet life, with Mannering worrying about the police because of those jewels. It's a straight deal, Mrs. Mannering, and you've got twenty-four hours to fix it. Mannering can sign cheques in prison, and you can get him to sign a blank cheque, and fill in the details afterwards. It will be a straightforward business arrangement, a purchase from an unknown collector—Mannering often does big deals like that, so it won't be remarkable. Will it?" He barked the question.

"No," Lorna made herself answer.

"So that's it, and all about it," said the driver. He had not turned his head once. "You get the money, sterling or dollars will be all the same to me, and you'll get instructions how to hand it over tomorrow afternoon. Don't tell anyone else about this. Just get Mannering to sign a blank cheque. Don't tell your lawyer friend, on a job like this, you couldn't rely on him. And remember this, Mrs. Em—if you don't come with the money when I tell you to, there won't be any witnesses, there won't be a chance in hell for Mannering. That clear?"

"Yes," she said, quite firmly.

"All right, you can go," the driver said. "You walk straight on here, turn right, and then you'll find yourself in Earl's Court Road, and you can take yourself home. Don't make any mistake, Mrs. Em—and don't imagine there's any way out, because my witnesses can talk two ways."

Lorna caught her breath.

"What do you mean?"

"They can swear that Farmer was banged over the head in the street, or they can swear they saw him going upstairs without anything wrong with him. They can be just the witnesses the police need to prove their case, see? I haven't worked this out to be beaten at the post. Either I get that money, or Mannering will be found guilty of killing Farmer up in your flat. There's no other choice."

The man next to Lorna leaned forward, pressed down the handle, and pushed open the door. After a moment she got out, awkwardly, and stumbled. The man made no attempt to help her. She stood in the dark street with the desolate stretch of land behind her, and felt terribly afraid. She heard the engine of the car start up, and began to walk the way the man had told her.

Then cars swung into the street at either end, headlights blazing, and two men sprang up from the waste land. One of them shouted:

"This way, Mrs. Mannering! This way!"

She spun round. She heard the roar of the Vauxhall's engine, and the whine of the other engines, and then heard a rending, crunching sound. She turned her head, and saw the Vauxhall heading towards her, already over the kerb. She flung herself to one side, caught her foot against some rubble, and pitched forward. A man shouted:

"Stop there! Police!"

The Vauxhall bumped over the waste land, and the two policeman who had been hiding there jumped to one side. The Vauxhall gathered speed. Lorna tried to pick herself up, but slipped again. Great lights were behind her, from the converging police cars. Men were jumping out of moving cars, and shouting. She saw seven or eight of them chasing after the Vauxhall, but it was going fast over the waste land towards the backs of the blocks of flats, and it had a hundred yards start.

Then two men came to help Lorna to her feet. One of them was Ingleby.

24

GOOD NEIGHBOURS

'So you had Lorna trailed by radio reports from police cars and police call boxes, and you converged on the car as soon as she'd got out," Mannering said bitterly. "And you'll try to persuade me that you thought that directly she was away from the car, she was clear of danger! This man who calls himself Smith will believe that she lied to him, that she knew the police were there. He'll kill her for it."

Bristow said: "That's simply looking on the gloomy side."

"Is it?" Mannering said. He felt viciously angry. "You lost Smith and his companion, and Lorna can't say what they looked like. She couldn't even swear to the identity of the coloured man who took her to Earl's Court."

"He can't help anyway," Bristow said. They were in the cell at Brixton, and Pleydell was sitting by, listening without making comment. "We picked him up—he was followed from the station. He swears that he doesn't know who Smith is or where he lives, he simply acted as a messenger. It was the coloured man who picked up the messages from Laker *alias* Klein at the Overseas Club, and he had precise instructions what to do last night, and just carried them out. When he first came to England from Jamaica he had a very rough time, committed several burglaries, and sold the stuff to this man Smith, through an intermediary. Then Smith blackmailed him into doing what he wanted."

"Can he identify Smith?"

"He says he's only seen him in the dark, and always when Smith was at the wheel of a car, so that he only saw his back."

"So Smith's as free as the air, with a hate for Lorna

and a fortune in jewels still stached away," Mannering declared.

"John," murmured Pleydell, "there are advantages, you know. After this, the police can't proceed with their charge. They'll have to withdraw it—I think I can persuade them to shorten the remand period, and to have a special hearing. Chittering was taken by train out to Wimbledon late last night and turned loose in the middle of Wimbledon Common, but his and all the other newspapers have the story, and it will be all over the front pages. And Bristow's men did make sure that Lorna came to no harm."

Mannering said gruffly: "If they'd handled this properly they could have caught the men." He stood in front of Bristow. "Haven't you any idea at all where to find them?"

"Not yet," Bristow admitted. "But until they're found, you and Lorna will have every protection."

"This chap might wait a year or more before he tries to get his own back," Mannering said roughly. "And you know it. He waited fifteen years to get those jewels, and now he's still got them on his hands. What I can't understand—"

He broke off.

The problem, as a problem, was pressing more heavily on his mind. His anger was fading, his fears for Lorna were in the future—certainly there was no immediate danger for her.

". . . is why they let Rebecca bring the fake jewels—and poor fakes at that. What did Lorna say? Laker as Klein checked that I wouldn't play with stolen jewels, and they were going to try again through the girl?"

"Yes."

"But they wouldn't get anywhere by sending me the fake jewels," Mannering protested. He began to walk about the cell, one hand in his pocket, the other clenched in front of him. "If they'd tried to persuade me to handle the real stuff, through Rebecca, it might have made some sense. If I'd once taken the job on for her, I would have been landed with the stolen jewels, and they might hope to make me keep selling them, by blackmailing me. But the fakes were pointless."

He broke off. Bristow was watching him closely, and Pleydell glanced at the Yard man, as much as to say: "It's coming."

Mannering felt a sudden warmth of excitement, an eagerness greater than he had known even when he had been told what had happened earlier in the night. Quite suddenly, he felt that he had at least half of the answer, and that it had been waiting for him to see. Every piece of information had its significance, and now he believed that he began to see the shape of the completed puzzle.

". . . Rebecca brought the jewels from her father," he said softly. "She believed them to be real, but—did *he*? After she had left for Quinns, he was murdered. Why? He must have known where his brother-in-law had been for the past fifteen years. He must have known that the jewels were not heirlooms, but were stolen property. Supposing he substituted the fakes? Supposing he refused to let Rebecca become involved? Supposing he threatened to give the secret away—the identity of Smith and the hiding place of the jewels—so as to protect her? That would explain his murder, wouldn't it?"

Bristow said softly: "It could."

"It certainly could," said Mannering, and his voice was harsh with growing excitement. "And if Rebecca's father was involved in this business, it could explain a great many things. Bill—someone got into his flat and killed him, and there were no signs of forced entry. Right?"

"Right."

"A man got into the flat again yesterday morning and attacked Rebecca, and then vanished without a trace. Right?"

Pleydell jumped up. "Good God!"

"Right," said Bristow, in a tense voice.

"Bill," Mannering said, "you haven't done a lot to

make me enthusiastic about you on this job, but here's a way you can make amends. Take me to Mapperley Street, Notting Hill. Take me to the Blests' flat. Let me search the place thoroughly—even if you've already been over it with a fine-tooth comb. Have as big a bodyguard as you like, but take it from me I won't try to escape this time. I would just like to be in at the showdown. You can get a suspect out of Brixton to take him back to the scene of the crime, can't you?"

"I should think I can," said Bristow. "Yes, of course I can. Who else do you want at the flat?"

"Rebecca, I'm afraid," said Mannering. "Lorna, too, because she might be able to identify either of last night's men. Young Terry McKay, of course, and Chittering. And if you really want Ingleby there, I'll forgive you." His eyes were very bright, and his heart was racing. "I might even forgive you for being a son of a so-and-so, after all."

. . . .

A few of the people of Mapperley Street saw the two police cars which drew up outside number 127, in the middle of that afternoon. Several windows went up, doors opened, more and more people came to see what was going on. No newspapers had been informed, and Chittering had been told off the record. He was already in the Blests' flat, with Lorna, Rebecca and young McKay. Mannering was helped out of the car by Ingleby, who had sat next to him throughout the journey. Two uniformed policemen were at the front door, which was open. Bristow and another Yard man came from the second car.

Just inside the hallway, moments later, Ingleby was standing with a large shallow box in his hands. In it was a piece of broken picture frame, and some tiny splinters of glass.

"From Larraby's picture," said Mannering keenly. "Where did you find those?"

"In the boot of a car parked outside," Ingleby said. "So someone here went to Larraby's flat."

They walked upstairs, heavily, and the door of the downstairs flat opened a few inches; the woman Ashton glanced through, then closed the door.

The door of the Blests' flat was also open, and a policeman was on duty.

"Well, now we're here, show us how you can search this flat better than we could," challenged Ingleby; there was still a note of sourness in his voice.

"Where do you want to start?" Bristow demanded.

Lorna was coming from the living-room, and Mannering did not answer Bristow, but looked at his wife, and smiled. He felt the glow of satisfaction which always came from realisation of her absolute loyalty, of the affection they had for each other, which could so easily have been taken for granted. He glanced from her to Rebecca, and to young McKay, who was looking stiff and awkward, as if alarmed. Chittering, with a bruise on his forehead and a bandage on his left hand, was sitting on the arm of a chair.

"Hallo, my sweet," Mannering said to Lorna. "It won't be long now, and for last night—just thanks." He turned to Bristow. "I don't think we need search up here, Bill. I think we should search downstairs, among the friends and neighbours. The neighbours could come in and out, remember—especially if they had a key. The neighbours were able to talk to Laker *alias* Klein whenever he was here with his brother. Laker had to talk to accomplices, yet none could be traced. Here's the one obvious rendezvous, and the obvious people are the Ashtons. Remember that apart from Terry McKay, the only people likely to know when Rebecca began to doubt whether she had seen the right jewels at the Yard—"

"Ruth Ashton!" exclaimed Rebecca. Her eyes held a glint of unbelief. "*Ruth?*"

"That's right," said Mannering. "Ruth Ashton—so Ashton would know that if he wanted to have me where he wanted me, he had to get rid of you as a witness. The raider came in without being heard, and disappeared most mysteriously. Out of one window and into another below—there can't be much doubt about that. Do you think there can, Bill?"

Ingleby said: "But we'd never given them a thought!"

"No, we hadn't, had we?" said Mannering. "May I come down with you?"

"Yes." Bristow said to Ingleby: "Go and call on the Ashtons. There's a complete cordon round the street, John. No one will get away this time."

"I hope not," said Mannering. "I don't think the Yard would ever live it down."

They stood waiting, as Ingleby and two others hurried down the stairs to the ground floor flat; there came a thudding on the door.

"Bill," Mannering went on, "let's have a grandstand view." Bristow led the way to the passage again, Mannering following him. Rebecca was talking in high-pitched whispers, and the name "*Ruth*" kept cropping up. Mannering looked down over the banisters, and saw Ingleby and the other man, Ingleby thumping on the door with a clenched fist, and calling:

"Open in the name of the law. Open this door!"

The woman answered in a quavering voice: "All right, all right." Ingleby and his man stood back, and Mannering saw the door open a crack. Because of his position, he could see better than Ingleby, and he was a split second ahead of Bristow in realising what was going on. The old woman was opening the door, and something bright glinted a foot or two above her head.

The man Ashton was there, holding a hammer.

"Look out!" Mannering cried, and as he shouted, the door opened wide and Ashton leapt forward, hammer sweeping towards Ingleby's head. Ingleby glanced up at Mannering, then dodged to one side. The hammer brushed on his shoulder, missing his head completely. Ashton turned desperately to attack the other Yard man, but as he struck, Mannering swung on to the banisters, slid down, then leapt to the passage floor. He banged bodily into Ashton, who had half turned to meet the new threat. He still held the hammer.

"*John!*" cried Lorna.

Mannering threw himself at the man, carrying him back several feet. The head of the hammer caught between two banister rails, and jerked Ashton's arm back. Ashton cried out in pain, and let go the hammer. As he stood there, swaying, Mannering pushed him back into the waiting arms of Ingleby and the other policeman.

. . . .

The other jewels were found under the floorboards in the flat below the Blests'.

By that time, Mrs. Ashton had admitted everything that was necessary, although Ashton—known now to be *alias* Smith—refused to say a word. He had been Laker's accomplice in the old days, and had waited until Laker had come out of prison. He and Laker had planned to dispose of the jewels between them, but had not been able to find a buyer except at a very low price. Laker had worked out the scheme to involve Quinns, hoping to pass the jewels off as being legitimately owned by African families. After Laker's death, his associates started to work through Rebecca, on the legacy pretext.

Samuel Blest, who had been prepared to help the associates himself, had not been willing to let them use his daughter, and had threatened to inform the police.

"That was an invitation to murder," Bristow said, later that evening. "According to Mrs. Ashton, Laker and Ashton had sets of imitation jewellery made years ago. Blest had always known about these. He substituted the fake gems for the real, so that Rebecca did not handle stolen jewels at all. He was a shrewd old man all right."

Lorna, sitting in a chair which had been brought into Mannering's cell, leaned forward and asked:

"What about Laker—how did he die?"

"Natural causes, beyond any doubt," said Bristow. "The

official death certificate called it cerebral haemorrhage. Ashton took over. Laker had made all the preparations, Ashton simply had to carry the job out. He used a young brute who hired himself out as a strong-arm man, and forced the coloured man to act as messenger. The drug given to Larraby was stolen from a chemist, when they first thought up the scheme. They wanted to wait for the moment to act, but Farmer precipitated the crisis. They forced him up to your flat at the point of a gun, and attacked him there. No doubt they stifled any cries he made—and the actual blows would make little sound. They left him for dead, but he was tougher than they realised. He actually managed to get to his feet. Incidentally, they kept Larraby alive, because they might want to use him again. They could always use a man at Quinns."

"What did happen to Larraby?" asked Pleydell.

"As far as we can make out, he was forced to open the strong-room under threat of death," Bristow answered. "When he was first attacked, in his flat, the picture by Wimperis was broken, and Ashton took it away and swept up the broken glass, rather than leave it there as evidence that Larraby had been subject to violence. Immediately after the strong-room job was finished, Larraby was given the drug. I'm told he will probably never remember what happened."

"That's good," approved Mannering. "The situation couldn't be much better."

"It could, a lot, "said Lorna. "You could be coming home tonight."

"Can't be done, I'm afraid," Bristow said regretfully. "But there will be a special hearing in the morning, and we shall submit no evidence, so there'll be no case to answer. The Press will have told the world about it before then, too."

"Bill," said Lorna, looking at him steadily.

"Yes?"

"Why did you go all out against John?"

"I've told him. I'll tell you," Bristow said. "I thought he

was playing the fool with those jewels. I thought he meant to sell them for Rebecca Blest. And I thought that he did kill Farmer in your flat—that's what all the evidence said."

"Go on like that," said Pleydell, "and you'll have us saying that we should never believe the evidence." He stood up. "Lorna, we ought to go, and let John spend his last night in jail in peace."

.   .   .   .

After a three-minute hearing, Mannering heard the magistrate, McKenzie-James, dismiss the case. He saw the magistrate's clerk frown in annoyance at the people crowded in the public gallery, who were applauding; even the men in the Press Box joined in.

Mannering went down into the well of the court; and joined Lorna. They went out together. Young McKay was waving to him enthusiastically with his right arm; his left was tight about Rebecca's waist. Chittering joined them at the door which led to the street, where at least a thousand people had gathered. There was a loud-voiced cheer when Mannering appeared.

Bristow and Ingleby were at the doorway.

"No Black Maria?" Mannering inquired.

"Mr. Mannering," said Ingleby.

"Yes?"

"I had to do what I conceived to be my duty."

"My dear chap," said Mannering. "I wouldn't expect less." He put out his hand, and Ingleby seemed both surprised and genuinely pleased.

"*Au revoir*, Bill," Mannering said. "When Lorna's really forgiven you, you must come and have a meal."

Pleydell came hurrying from the court, saying:

"John, I'm told there's a plane leaving London Airport for New York in an hour's time with a seat vacant. I'll just about catch it, and I'll be away for two or three months. Try to keep out of trouble until I'm back."

"I'll keep him out of trouble," Lorna said.